TRUST BETRAYED

BY

RICHARD WRENN

I dedicate this work to my beautiful, darling wife, Denise, who has given me four lovely children, Emily, Alex, Edward and Victoria and a wonderfully happy and exciting life.

Disclaimer

This is a work of fiction. None of the characters or institutions portrayed in this novel are in any way based on real people or banks or other organisations and any similarity is purely coincidental.

Acknowledgements

Cover design by Eddie Wrenn.

I am indebted to my daughter Emily Harris for her assistance in editing this novel.

TRUST BETRAYED

CHAPTER ONE

July 1979

"I call you my Valentine." Graham Mitcham looked up uncertainly at the tall, thin, bespectacled spinster who had just addressed him. Sixty years old, Miss Turvey had been with the firm since leaving school, and he doubted whether she had ever been in love. "Why?" he asked. "Because you joined the firm on Saint Valentine's day," she replied primly and swept out of the room.

Mitcham reflected on this. Saint Valentine's days had never meant much to him, but he realised that he had indeed joined the firm of Williams Brown & Buller on Saint Valentine's day three years previously. Much had happened in that time. The firm, with an illustrious history spanning some two hundred years, had then been in serious decline, but now had recovered, largely due to the strenuous efforts of himself and his senior partner John Buller. Old partners had retired, and he and Buller had worked assiduously in modernising the firm, scrapping outmoded systems and introducing new technology. Such improvements had been resented by the senior staff, who had had to learn new skills. And no one had been more vociferous in opposing the changes than Miss Turvey, the senior clerk, for whom the change of the firm's name from Williams Brown & Buller to Buller & Mitcham had been the last straw.

'So, was this remark the sign of a thaw in relations?'
Mitcham mused.

His musing was interrupted by a knock on the door,
and in entered John Buller. Some thirty years older
than Mitcham, Buller was a tall, balding, courteous
man with a kindly disposition. Buller had been a
partner with the firm for many years and had resigned
himself to being part of a legal practice in decline
until the unexpected arrival of the youthful Mitcham.
Mitcham, then 26 years old, had decided that he did
not want to pursue his legal career in the City, and,
spotting an advertisement in the Law Society's
Gazette for a young solicitor to succeed old partners
who wished to retire from a country practice in the
Midlands, had applied for the post. A perfunctory
interview with the then Senior Partner had led to
Mitcham's appointment. So, it was on Saint
Valentine's day, three years before, that Mitcham had
been introduced to Buller. Although Buller was
much older than himself, Mitcham liked and
respected his partner, who had quickly acceded to
Mitcham's plans to revive the practice. He knew very
little about him as Buller lived in Roystrop, a
neighbouring town which was some ten miles away,
and he was quite reserved and did not seem to
entertain at home. Miss Turvey had told him that
Buller was a widower, whose wife, Marjorie, had
died some years previously, leaving him with an
adolescent daughter to bring up. Marjorie's demise
had apparently brought Buller a substantial
inheritance.

2

"Graham," his partner intoned. "I wonder if you could handle a case for me. I obviously cannot do it because the client is my daughter." "Of course," replied Mitcham. "Are you sure that you want me to handle it? What is it about?" Mitcham looked enquiringly at Buller. "I think it best if I leave it to Susan to tell you," Buller responded. "Susan can come to see you whenever it is convenient for you. You can reach her on this telephone number." He handed Mitcham a scrap of paper and left the room.

Mitcham reached for the telephone and dialled the number on the piece of paper. "Hello. Susan Buller speaking," a calm, charming voice replied. "Hello, Miss Buller. Graham Mitcham speaking. Your father says that you would like to see me over some problem. When would you like to come in?"

An appointment was made for the following afternoon and Mitcham replaced the phone in its holder, wondering what the nature of the problem would be.

"Mr. Mitcham. There is a lady here asking to see you. Her name is Miss Buller. Shall I send her up?" Mitcham arose from his chair. "Yes, please do, Jane. I will meet her at the top of the stairs," Mitcham instructed.

Mitcham left his room and walked to the top of the stairs. To his surprise, he saw a tall, attractive, smartly dressed brunette pause at the bottom of the staircase and then start to ascend the staircase. Reminding himself that the young lady was a client and also his partner's daughter, Mitcham assumed a professional air. "Miss Buller. It is very nice to meet you. Please come this way." He ushered her into his room and pulled up a chair for her in front of his desk. "Your father has occasionally mentioned his daughter to me so it is very nice to be able to put a face to a name," he said as he ushered her into the chair. Susan blushed a little, and Mitcham hurriedly moved on. "How can I help you?" he inquired, seating himself into his chair behind his desk.

Susan hesitated, and took a deep breath. "The Police want to prosecute me for failing to stop at a zebra crossing." "Oh!" exclaimed Mitcham, scrutinising his new client. "Have they issued a Summons against you?" He looked quizzically at Susan as she picked up her handbag from the floor and fumbled through it. A good-looking girl, he thought, surmising that she was in her early to mid-twenties. Buller had certainly kept her hidden from him. Susan produced a piece of paper issued by the Police. He scanned it quickly. It summonsed her for failing to stop at a zebra crossing when a lollipop lady had stepped on to the zebra crossing holding up a halt sign. "Did you receive a Notice of Intended Prosecution?" asked Mitcham. Again, Susan delved into her handbag and produced a piece of paper. "H'mm. That seems to be in order," commented Mitcham: "What do you have to say about it?"

4

Susan flinched. "I do not know anything about it," she replied. "The zebra crossing is opposite the school at the bottom of our road and I must drive through it several times a day. I do not remember any occasion when a lollipop lady stepped into the road and I carried on driving." She looked uncomfortable, Mitcham thought as he wrote down her words on a sheet of paper. He looked again at the words in the Summons and the Statement of Facts. It stated that the defendant was driving a Ford Fiesta motor car registration number HRP 545. "Is that your car?" he asked. "Yes," replied Susan. "And were you living at your Father's home on that day?" He referred to the date in the Summons. "Yes" was the answer.

Mitcham sat back in his chair and studied his client. This was going to be difficult he mused to himself. He tried to visualise the zebra crossing having driven along his partner's road a couple of times in the past three years, the first time out of curiosity to see where and in what type of house his partner lived. He recalled a large Victorian detached house with a small front garden, with the paint work coloured brown. Slightly forlorn, he shuddered. Still in these cases one never knew how the evidence would play out, and if his client was adamant that she knew nothing about her alleged offence and wished to plead "Not guilty" he would have to do his best to get her acquitted. He would still have preferred her to plead "Guilty" and ask him to plead in mitigation for her. A much easier task. He rocked in his chair, gazing at her. "And how do you wish to plead?" he asked, almost as an afterthought. "Oh! Not guilty, of

5

course," she replied confidently. "Oh dear!" he thought. Still it would give him a chance to get to know her better.

"How did you get on with my partner, Susan?" Buller enquired of his daughter at dinner that evening. "Oh, very well," his daughter answered brightly. "He was very professional and seemed to believe me. He is going to make some enquiries of the Prosecution and we have arranged to meet again on Friday afternoon to discuss what he has found out." Buller looked sympathetically at his daughter. "Oh, Graham is very good. You are in safe hands – he has a very good track record. Only the other day he secured an acquittal in what appeared to be a hopeless case, only because the Prosecution had failed to prepare the prosecution case properly." He looked at his daughter who beamed at him. "You did not tell me that he was so young and handsome," she teased her father accusingly. "I always assumed that he was middle aged." Buller appraised his daughter. 'So like her mother,' he reflected. 'Not slow in coming forward. And she has her looks, so attractive, yet an intelligent looking face. Men will find her very desirable,' he ruminated as he had done many times in the past. 'A pity that she is so determined to pursue a medical career.' He had done his best to dissuade her from becoming a doctor believing that it was too demanding a career, but she had been determined to do so. His daughter had just qualified as a doctor and was excitingly waiting to start her first

6

paid post as a junior doctor at St. Peter's hospital in London. 'Perhaps she will learn that there are other worthwhile pursuits than saving lives,' he reflected.

For Buller was devoted to his daughter. The death of his loving wife, Marjorie, some nine years before, from throat cancer had been a tragedy for him. He had nursed her for several years before her final illness, and it took a long time for him to recover from his bereavement. He sought solace in caring for Susan, who had been devastated by the loss of her mother. Each recognised, more than ever before, that they needed each other and each other's love and support. But after a while Buller had come to realise that the increasing demands of his professional life prevented him from devoting the time and attention that his energetic, fourteen years' old daughter required, and that he was also unsuited to the task of bringing up his daughter. A mother's guidance and influence were lacking. He felt inadequate as a surrogate mother. Besides, he was anxious to resume full participation in the masonic activities of his Lodge and the social life of Menston Rotary Club of which he was a Past President.

Reluctantly, he came to the conclusion that her needs would be better fulfilled at a boarding school for girls, and he was fortunate that Royston was home to a well-respected public school where girls were accepted as weekly boarders. So, much against her wishes, Susan found herself attending Royston Public School for Girls as a weekly boarder. At first, she did not settle in to her new routine. She resented having to board, and being parted from the comfort and security of her home and her friends. She detested the routine of boarding school. But as the months passed, she settled in to the rhythm of her new existence, and began to make new friends among her class mates. The school posed new challenges for her, and she began to thrive. Inspiring teachers stimulated her interest in scientific subjects, and she discovered that she had an innate feeling for scientific principles and procedures. Biology particularly absorbed her interest. Hard work followed, and she devoted herself to study, finding it absorbing and fulfilling. It also distracted her from mourning the loss of her mother and the absence during the week of her father, with whom she was reunited every weekend. But the school also introduced her to the challenge of playing tennis, and she found that she had a natural aptitude for the game, which the school was keen to develop. And so, she spent her free hours on the school's tennis courts, honing her skills and learning the techniques and tactics of the game. Four years later outstanding "A" level results led to a place for Susan at London University to read medicine. Buller was very proud of her, and very relieved that she had emerged from grief and adolescence as a well-balanced, highly motivated, young lady.

"Officer, I am instructed to represent a Miss Susan Buller who is due to appear in Menston Magistrates' Court on Wednesday the 18th of July charged with failing to stop at a zebra crossing when being directed to do so by a lollipop lady. I wonder, please, if you could read out to me the prosecution witness statements so that I can decide how to advise my client." Mitcham waited patiently as the officer extracted and opened a thin file. She found the case notes and read out the lollipop lady's statement. It seemed that normally the lollipop lady would not have taken any action, but, in this case, she was some two yards on to the zebra crossing trying to restrain a gaggle of excited schoolchildren from rushing across the road when a blue Ford Fiesta driven by a young lady driver sped across the other side of the road, blatantly ignoring her "Halt" sign and the danger inherent in the situation. It had happened so fast, and she had had to give her full attention to the children, that she had not noted the registration number. But a police officer had been nearby and had seen the incident and had noted down the car registration number, so she had felt constrained to accede to his suggestion that the driver should be prosecuted. The police officer's statement corroborated the lollipop lady's evidence. He had seen the whole incident, noted down the car registration number in his notebook and had obtained the name and address of the car's registered owner from the DVLC. Enquiry of the registered owner established that the only person who had driven that car on that day was a Miss Susan Buller. So, he had arranged for a Notice of Intended Prosecution to be sent to her. "Thank you, officer" Mitcham said with a sigh, "you have been most helpful."

13th July

"Are you sure that you want to plead Not Guilty?"
Mitcham asked his demure client at the resumed
meeting on Friday afternoon. He had looked forward
to the prospect of meeting his new client with a
mixture of excitement and foreboding. Carefully he
had reported to her the contents of the police evidence
against her and explained the difficulties which he
would encounter in trying to upset what he regarded
as a watertight case against her. Her response,
however, was adamant. Buoyed by her father's
positive assessment of Mitcham's advocacy talent and
her own determination to prove her innocence, she
asserted, "I have no doubt of my innocence, Mr
Mitcham. I have no recollection of the incident, and
it is my practice always to slow down and if
necessary to stop at that zebra crossing. There must
have been some mistake by the Police. I do want to
prove my innocence, Mr. Mitcham." Mitcham
appraised her. She certainly had character, he
reflected, as he showed her out of his room. "I will
see you, then, outside the Magistrates Court on
Wednesday morning, 18th July, at, shall we say, 10
o'clock," he said at the top of the stairs. "Right, Mr.
Mitcham and thank you for all your help and advice,
but I do want to fight it." She looked imploringly at
him.

Wednesday 18ᵗʰ July

Mitcham arrived early at the Court. He had notified
the Court office the previous week that his client
wished to plead "Not guilty" and had been told that
the Police witnesses were available for that day, and
that the case would be listed for hearing that morning.
He hovered at the top of the steps leading into the
drab Victorian Court building, waiting for his client
to arrive.

Susan arrived promptly at 10 o'clock, looking nervous
and less self-assured, Mitcham noted. "You still have
time to change your plea if you wish to," Mitcham
told her as soon as they entered the small, dingy,
conference room. "No, Mr. Mitcham, I have not
changed my mind. I am resolved to contest the
summons." "Well," said Mr. Mitcham, "Remember
that when you are in the witness box, to keep your
answers short and to the point. Too many people say
too much in the witness box and dig a hole for
themselves." Susan smiled at his casual language.
Perhaps there was a lighter side to his character than
he had yet revealed. She hoped that she would one
day find out.

Mitcham surveyed the court room. He had performed
there on many occasions and was familiar with most
of the magistrates and the Court Clerk, Benting. He
had not met the Prosecuting Solicitor before. Mr.
Jervis was a young, earnest type, he thought, probably

11

recently qualified and in his first job. He gazed up with some dismay at the bench where three magistrates were sitting. Sat between a lady magistrate, whom he did not know, and a middle-aged man was Mr. Craddock, whom he did not like. Mr. Craddock was an accountant by profession, but relished his public office as Chairman of the Menston magistrates bench. He was sharp, and enjoyed being caustic when he had the chance. "Oh dear!" thought Mitcham, "this is going to be a difficult morning." Susan had been ushered by the Court Usher into the dock, feeling embarrassed and stressed at the ordeal that lay ahead. "No going back now," she steeled herself as she gazed at the back of Mitcham's head.

Benting called the Court to order. "The Police against Miss Susan Buller." he announced. "Are you Miss Susan Buller?" he asked gravely. "Yes" came a less than confident reply. "Mr. Jervis, if you would like to present the Prosecution case." "Very well, Sir," Mr Jervis replied as he rose to his feet. Jervis gave a short, confident speech presenting the case that the Prosecution expected to prove in evidence. He would be calling two witnesses: the first, the lollipop lady who would explain what had happened, and then the police officer who had observed the incident and had made enquiries of the DVLC to identify the driver. He called the first witness, a bubbly, overweight middle-aged woman, who was far from bashful as she gave her evidence. Mitcham wrote down her evidence in furious shorthand, concentrating at the same time on the content of the evidence being given. "Your chance to cross examine the witness, Mr Mitcham," said Benting severely. Mitcham paused for a moment. He had a choice to make. Should he seek to challenge the accuracy or the veracity of the evidence which had been so confidently given? If that came to nought, he would simply have irritated the magistrates to no avail. On the other hand, he noted that the lollipop lady had not in her evidence identified his client. Perhaps better not to challenge her evidence. He rose slowly to his feet.

"No questions," he replied. Benting looked sharply at him; Craddock grunted. Susan looked askance at Mitcham. She had expected him to tear into the witness and pull her evidence apart in a glorious, incisive display of cross examination, not a meek "No questions". Perhaps her father had misrepresented his ability. Perhaps it would have been better to instruct a solicitor from another firm to represent her. How embarrassing this was all going to be for her.

Jervis called the police officer. A tall, upright young man, he was somewhat nervous in answering the questions that Jervis put to him. He had observed the incident, and was horrified that the young lady driver had failed to stop when the lollipop lady was standing some two yards inside the zebra crossing holding up a Halt sign with a crowd of excited, pushing children behind her. He had approached the lollipop lady, who was equally cross about what had happened, and had taken a full statement from her, which he then proceeded to read out. He had noted down the registration number of the blue Ford Fiesta which was being driven by a young lady with brown hair. He had then made enquiries of the DVLC and established that a John Buller was the registered owner. The Police had issued the statutory enquiry form to establish the name and address of the driver of the car on that occasion, and on receiving the information had issued a summons. "Thank you, Officer. That will be all." Jervis sat down with a flourish.

Mitcham stared at his notes in disbelief. Was he imagining it or had the Prosecution failed to identify his client as the driver of the Ford Fiesta? He hurriedly read through his scribbled notes, with mounting excitement. No, there had been no identification. To cross examine now would open the opportunity for identification, at the very least give the Prosecution the opportunity to identify his client in re-examination. Better not to give them the chance, he thought, conscious that the magistrates were growing restless at his delay.

"Mr. Mitcham, if you please," Benting prompted. Mitcham rose slowly to his feet. "No cross examination," he announced, to be greeted by a gasp from his client and a grunt from Craddock. "Mr. Jervis will you be calling any more witnesses?" asked Benting. "No," replied Jervis confidently. "So, that is the close of the Prosecution case," ruled Benting. "Yes, Sir," said Jervis and sat down, quietly relieved that the case had gone so well.

Benting completed his notes, scratched his chin and asked Mitcham to open the defence. Susan, in

14

dismay, watched Mitcham get to his feet. "What a let-down!" she thought. A frisson of excitement flowed through Mitcham as he cleared his throat. Such an elementary mistake had been made by Jervis that he could not believe his luck. Surely, he must be correct. Surely this could not backfire. Were Benting's notes accurate and comprehensive? It was all a bit of a gamble.

"There is no case for my client to answer," he declared as confidently as he could muster. He was conscious of a stirring around the Court and a caustic grunt from Craddock. "In their evidence, the Prosecution failed to identify the defendant as the driver of the car. I invite Your Worships to dismiss the case." As he resumed his seat he glanced at Jervis who, red faced, was flipping quickly through his notes. The Police Inspector by his side was gazing in disbelief at the ceiling. "Court will rise," commanded Benting as the magistrates stood up and retired to their conference room.

Susan was confused. Anger at Mitcham's inept performance had been consumed by bewilderment at the change of events. Did this mean that she was after all in the clear? Oh, she did hope so. But what would happen if the magistrates rejected Mitcham's argument? What then? The range of emotions which had traversed through her body were too much to bear. Oh, why had she been so rash as to insist on pleading not guilty? She could have saved herself all this trauma and expense by pleading guilty by letter through the post.

15

Mitcham too was feeling apprehensive. "What if the magistrates rejected his submission?" he thought balefully, as he watched Benting rise to his feet, having been summoned by the magistrates to advise them on a point of law. Was there any point in calling Susan to give evidence when he had so signally failed to challenge the prosecution evidence? To expose her to the humiliation of the witness box? And if she were then found guilty, what would she think of him? What prospect would there be of developing a friendship with her after what would seem to her to have been such a limp performance? He shuddered. Best not to call her to give evidence, he reassured himself, but to challenge the magistrates to convict or acquit her on the submission that he had made.

The minutes ticked by. The tension in the Court was unmistakable. Twenty minutes passed before the magistrates filed back into the Court and sat down. Craddock whispered down to Benting. Benting nodded. Craddock looked severely down from the Bench at Mitcham. "Case dismissed," he announced sharply, aware of the registering of surprise among the people gathered before him.

The defendant gasped. As Jervis slumped back in his chair, the Police Inspector involuntarily slammed his fist on the table before him. "Order in Court," shouted Benting. "Miss Buller, you are free to go."

Bewildered by the sudden change of events, and

conscious that all eyes were on her, Susan rose unsteadily to her feet and stepped down from the dock. Uncertain in which direction she should go, she was relieved to find Mitcham take her elbow and guide her from the room. Outside the Court room she slumped heavily against Mitcham as her legs felt giddy. "Does this mean that I am acquitted?" she gasped. "Yes," replied Mitcham. "It is all over. The case has been dismissed – thrown out of Court," he added unnecessarily, enjoying his relief that it was all so successfully over. "Let's go and find a coffee." "And celebrate," responded Susan, regaining her poise. Outside the Court building she turned excitedly to Mitcham and, in an impulse, threw her arms around him and kissed him on the cheek.

Taken aback by her embrace, Mitcham repeated, "Let's go and find a coffee." Seated in a small, dingy coffee shop opposite the Courthouse, Susan, feeling elated, gingerly stretched her hand forward to touch Mitcham's hand and asked, "Graham. I can call you Graham now that this horrid business is over, can't I?" Mitcham nodded appreciatively. "I am so enormously grateful to you. I cannot believe it is all over! I do hope that we can meet again." "Game, set and match," reflected Mitcham as he watched a dejected Jervis walk forlornly past the shop window. "Poor blighter, how awful for him!" Mitcham reflected.

CHAPTER TWO

"Graham?" Mitcham looked up from the papers on his desk as his partner entered the room. "Susan has told me of your success today. Thank you so much for what you did for her. She wants us all to go out for dinner to celebrate her acquittal. I cannot manage tonight, but are you free tomorrow? I suggest that we all go to The Falcon at, say, 8 o'clock, if that is okay with you?" Then, as an afterthought, he added archly, "If you don't mind, I should like to bring Elspeth, my lady friend of some years, along to join us. She would love to join in the celebration." "I would love to," replied Mitcham, hurriedly adding that it would be a pleasure to meet Elspeth.

"Good, see you at 8 o'clock at The Falcon then." With that, his senior partner slipped out of the room. "You sly, old man," thought Mitcham as the door closed behind Buller. "Fancy keeping your girlfriend secret all these years!"

19th July

The following evening Mitcham arrived promptly at The Falcon, a thatched restaurant in a nearby village which was highly rated in the County for the quality of its cuisine. An aged Daimler pulled up in the car park, and out climbed an excited Susan with her father and a matronly, dark haired woman in her wake. To the surprise of her father, Susan ran across to Graham and threw her arms around him in a big hug. She kissed him on the cheek, much to Graham's delight and embarrassment. Extricating himself from her embrace, Mitcham grinned awkwardly at his partner and lady friend. "Let me introduce you to Elspeth," Buller beckoned Elspeth rather formally towards him, before marching off in the direction of the restaurant entrance.

The dinner that followed was a slightly restrained affair. Susan gushed excitedly about her success the day before, describing how Mitcham had dazzled and confounded the court with his skilled advocacy. Mitcham felt embarrassed, and was relieved when the subject turned to her future plans. He learned that she had just passed her medical finals at London University and had secured a placement at St Peter's Hospital in London as a junior house doctor, which assignment would begin in September. She had celebrated her success by spending two weeks touring France with a girlfriend in her Ford Fiesta. Her ambition was to become a General Practitioner. Mitcham greeted this information with some foreboding. To conduct a relationship with her in London would, he knew, be difficult. The working hours and demanding shifts for junior house doctors were well recognised, making it difficult to arrange dates, and besides she would be surrounded by young house doctors who would find her very attractive. Perhaps he had better calm down, he thought. There may be no future in this.

He learned of the death of her mother some years

previously from throat cancer. Her father had taken a long time to recover from the loss of his wife. But then he had been introduced to Elspeth Shaw, a widow, who lived in Menston and whom he had vaguely known in his youth. They had found one another attractive, and had begun at first a platonic relationship which had developed into something deeper. Elspeth had kept her own home in Menston, but she and Buller would go on holiday together, enjoying the pleasure and solace of each other's company. They shared one past experience in common. They had discovered that they had both spent their respective honeymoons at the Imperial Hotel in Salcombe in Devon, and this hotel had become a favourite watering hole for both of them.

As the evening progressed Susan hinted that she would like Mitcham to drive her home. Mitcham was only too happy to acquiesce, reminding himself, however, that Susan was the daughter of his partner. He had better be careful about how he played this; there was much to lose if he overplayed his opportunity.

The journey back to his partner's house was largely uneventful. Susan sought to delve into his background, learning that his father had encouraged him to read Law at university and that he had managed to secure a place at Cambridge University. But he had found the subject depressingly laborious, and had often wondered if he would have found it more intellectually satisfying to have read History instead. But his father had discouraged him from changing courses, advising that History only offered careers in teaching or the Civil Service whilst the law opened up so many career options in law and in business. So, he had persevered, only to find later that preparation for his solicitors' final examinations was even more mind numbingly tedious. Having passed the examinations, two years of laborious training in Articles with a leading London firm of Solicitors ensued, after which he was admitted to the Roll of Solicitors. On qualifying he had decided to give the practice of the Law a two years' trial period, and so he had stayed on as an assistant solicitor with the firm to which he had been articled.

But to his surprise he had found that practice, whilst very stressful, was fascinating and stimulating, and sometimes exciting. After a while, though, he had realised that he had no wish to spend his career working in a city. He found that he did not like living in the hustle and bustle, dirt, noise and pollution of London, despite its many attractions. So, after two years he decided to eschew working in London and opted instead for a working life in a big town in the Midlands. Susan prised out of him why he had joined her father's firm. He confided that he had realised that there was potential in rescuing an old established firm in decline where he could quickly become a leading equity partner. He had not wanted to be in a large firm where one worked up the career ladder to become an equity partner in a large equity partnership, buffeted by the demands of his peers.

Instead he wanted to be in charge of the development of his career, to be his own boss. He found that he liked Menston, a town with a lively, sociable community, large enough to support a shopping centre and several light industrial estates with an interesting array of large and small businesses. This promised to provide considerable work for the firm of Buller & Mitcham.

He revealed all this grudgingly as he was talking to his senior partner's daughter and was not at all certain that he wanted her to report all this to her father. But under some probing pressure he had confessed it. Besides, he added, a small practice like Buller & Mitcham offered a much wider range of legal work than would be open to him in a larger practice, where specialism was the order of the day. Nor had he regretted joining the firm, once the old partners had retired and he was able to introduce modern technology and procedures into the firm. He liked working with her father whom he greatly respected. And besides, the people of Menston threw up the most extraordinary array of problems, which were deeply satisfying to solve. In short, it served his fertile mind very well. Susan listened to him avidly.

On arriving at her father's house, Mitcham noticed that the bedroom light was on. Waiting up for the safe and chaste return of his daughter Mitcham reflected ruefully. Buller no doubt harboured the same misgivings about a relationship developing between his daughter and his partner as Mitcham had warned himself about. The potential for catastrophe of any kind was there. He switched off the engine and turned to look at his passenger. To his surprise her eyes were shining brightly at him, as her right hand reached for his. Pulling him towards her, she sought his lips, opened her lips and passionately kissed him. "Oh well," Mitcham thought, casting caution aside. "This is a risk I very much want to take." Her father's bedroom light stayed on for much longer than he wanted.

Susan detached herself from Mitcham's embrace. Bidding him "Goodnight" she kissed him again, and then let herself out of the car. "I very much want to see you again, Graham. Do, please, give me a ring soon. I can't wait to go out with you on our own," she implored. "I will," promised Mitcham, "I certainly will." He watched her run up the drive to the front door and let herself in. The bedroom light went out.

Mitcham drove slowly back to Menston in a state of excitement and confusion. He had expected the evening to be a quiet, formal affair, lightened by the presence of Susan. He had not expected it to lead to kissing and embracing Susan, nor had he intended to reveal so much about himself to her. It had all happened very quickly, excitingly so. An unaccustomed sense of romance swept through him, tinged by a feeling of guilt that he was doing something that he should not be doing and which could have unfortunate repercussions. As he drove into the outskirts of Menston his mind was still in a whirl of confusion. He stopped his car in the Market Square, and climbed out. He needed some fresh air to calm his exhilaration and some gentle exercise to compose himself.

The Market Square was dominated by the majestic, medieval spire of Saint Swithun's Parish Church. On the opposite side of the Square stood the somewhat gaunt Victorian building which housed the offices of Buller and Mitcham. Mitcham stood for a while by the Market Cross in the middle of the Square gazing at his offices. This was where he had planned his future. What would his future be? He strolled around the Square lost in reverie until tiredness interrupted his thoughts and he returned to his car to continue his drive home to his flat.

In her bed, Susan found that she was too excited to sleep. Her mind was racing through the events of the past two days. Her father had explained how perspicacious Graham had been in assessing the evidence given by the prosecution witnesses in the heat of the moment and what nerves of steel he had to pursue the strategy he had followed. Susan had felt guilty that she had so misjudged his skill during the trial, regretting that she had ever doubted him. And he was so handsome, she reflected, as she recalled his aquiline features, dark hair and strong build. "I am beginning to fall in love with him," she thought dreamily. She then reflected on the events of the evening and her final hot embrace with him in his car.

She, too, had noted that her father's bedroom light was on throughout the period that they had remained in the car, and that it had only been extinguished when she opened the front door of the house. She hoped that her father was not going to be difficult over her seeing Graham. What a pity it was that her father had taken up with Elspeth, whom she did not particularly like. Still, as long as he was happy and they did not marry, she could put up with the relationship. But marriage would be a different matter. Marriage! She drifted off to sleep dreaming that marriage to Graham would be a different matter altogether, altogether a different matter.

CHAPTER THREE

8th August 1979

"Damn!" exclaimed Mitcham. "Double fault!" chirped his young opponent from the other side of the net. Mitcham had a tendency to hit too hard through his serve and either mistimed impact or over served with the inevitable consequence that the ball did not enter the court.

A social tennis player, Mitcham had joined Menston Lawn Tennis Club for social rather than competitive tennis. Not so his opponent, who was an accomplished tennis player and who played regularly for the Ladies' first team when at home and who could hold her own against most tennis players at the Club of either sex. Mitcham knew that he was being outclassed.

"Better try to play her at golf," he thought, at which he was certainly better, before reflecting that she might be good at that too. Certainly, she was a good games player.

Half an hour later, hopelessly outclassed, Mitcham graciously conceded defeat. "How about a drink," he suggested hopefully. "Oh, Graham. That will be so nice, but would you rather not play another game?" she teased him. "Definitely not" was the firm reply.

Later that evening, in his car and on firmer ground, Mitcham kissed his new-found girlfriend. To his delight, Susan responded ardently.

At breakfast next morning, her father quizzed her on
her developing relationship. Was it wise for her to be
getting so involved with Graham when she was about
to start a strenuous year of work as a junior house
doctor at a leading London hospital he had asked.
"Oh, Dad!" was her response. "I am only enjoying a
fling, a bit of fun before I go to London." Her father
had grimaced, and a frown then developed over his
forehead as he buried himself in his Times
newspaper. "Well, be careful. He is my partner,"
was his parting response.

Later that evening, over a drink in the Golden Lion,
she reported the conversation to Graham. Graham
flinched on hearing this. Was this all that it was?
Speculating on what was passing through his mind,
Susan leaned towards him and kissed him gently on
the cheek. "That was what I told my father to keep
him at bay," she said. "But it is not what I think. I
am falling in love with you, and want you in my life."
Mitcham relaxed. "Thank God," he thought.

After he had dropped Susan off at her home and noted
that the bedroom light turned off as Susan let herself
in through the front door, Mitcham drove back to his
flat in Menston. As he did so he analysed his
relationship with Susan. Was she really falling in

love with him? Or was she just enjoying a holiday romance with him before starting her professional career at St. Peter's Hospital? He fervently hoped it was the former. Certainly, her whole behaviour towards him suggested that she was falling in love with him. Her constant searching for information about him, his family and his career suggested that she was in love with him, involving herself emotionally in his life. And there was no holding back in her loving of him. Her kissing and embracing was hot, intense and passionate. In fact, exciting. But could this be equally true of a holiday romance? After all they had only been going out together for three weeks, and there were still some four weeks to go before Susan returned to London. He told himself that he would have to be patient and see how events unfurled. But his partner was obviously disturbed about the relationship, and concerned about the possible fallout if the relationship ended on bad terms. Mitcham sighed. Perhaps he was seeking too much.

August melted into September, perhaps too quickly for Mitcham. He noted that Susan was becoming more excited about starting her medical career, and planning her new life in London. He felt apprehensive that the relationship may have peaked. But there had been no evidence of that. In fact, quite to the contrary. Susan had developed the routine of cooking dinner for Mitcham at his flat, much to the chagrin of her father who had enjoyed having his evening meal prepared for himself at home. Susan had even decorated Mitcham's living room with a regular supply of cut flowers; and only the other day she had presented Mitcham with a silver framed photograph of herself which she had placed on his bedside table, remarking that it would be the first face he would see when he woke up in the morning. 'And the last face when he went to bed at night,' he reflected. She had invited him to watch her play tennis for the first team against a neighbouring club only the last Saturday, and he had enjoyed the pleasure of watching her as she proceeded to beat her opponent. And whenever he returned her to her home after an evening out, he noted that the bedroom light would be extinguished when Susan entered the front door. 'How curious?' Mitcham had thought.

As the final weeks passed by, Susan asked Mitcham for a photograph of himself so that she could keep it by her bedside. Feeling slightly embarrassed, Mitcham had presented himself at an appointment at a photographic studio for that purpose, explaining to the photographer, as if it were necessary, that it was not an exercise in narcissism but a gift for his girlfriend. Susan had been thrilled when he had given the framed portrait to her, throwing her arms around him and giving him a big kiss. Hugging the picture to her chest, she exclaimed that it was her most prized possession which she would always treasure. So perhaps, he told himself, he was worrying unnecessarily.

Buller locked the front door as the two partners left the office for the night. They had just interviewed a young solicitor who had applied for their office vacancy, and had decided that she was most suitable for the probate post that they had in mind. Probate and trust work had been expanding, and neither felt that they wished to specialise in that time-consuming field. A reflection of how the firm was reviving under their stewardship, Mitcham reflected. As the key turned in the lock, Buller suddenly remarked: "Susan is quite besotted with you, you know." Mitcham was taken aback by the suddenness of the change in topic, and the subject of the remark. Until then they had been discussing the new appointment and the consequential adjustments to work load. Mitcham stiffened and he could feel a slight blush in his countenance. "I do hope that your relationship with my daughter is not going to come to grief. It would cause you and me some difficulty, you know." Mitcham nodded silently. Was his partner warning him off his daughter, and if so why? Did he regard him as unsuitable for his daughter, or mistrusted Mitcham's motives? Or was he simply concerned to preserve the happy and successful working relationship that had developed between Mitcham and himself, and was concerned about the impact, financial and personal, which would follow a breakdown in his relationship with Susan? Perhaps Buller had witnessed his daughter being infatuated with another man, only to cool suddenly in her feelings. All these thoughts flooded in an instant through his troubled mind. "Do not worry," was his immediate response. Ambivalent response, they both thought.

September

To his dismay, Buller learned that Susan had asked
Mitcham to drive her and all her belongings to her
new accommodation in the hostel adjoining St.
Peters's Hospital. Susan explained that in this way
Graham would be able to familiarise himself with the
layout of the hostel and the hospital and, besides, her
father would be spared the labour of carrying her
belongings from his car to her room. Buller was not
sure that he was being told the whole truth of the
thinking behind the arrangement, but had bowed to
the inevitable. Besides, Susan reasoned, everything
would be in place for his visit the following weekend.
Buller sadly telephoned Elspeth to tell her the news
and to postpone the weekend in London that he had
promised her. He then telephoned the London hotel
and two restaurants to rearrange his bookings for the
following weekend.

Susan had noticed her father's disappointment with
her decision to ask Mitcham to settle her into her new
accommodation. She had not wished to upset her
father, whom she loved dearly, but she did want
Mitcham to drive her to London and to help her to
move into her new home. She was also excited at the
prospect of showing Mitcham around St. Peter's
Hospital and spending the first weekend there with
him. Besides that, she knew that her father was
planning to take Elspeth with him and staying on with
her in London for the weekend. She did not like

Elspeth sufficiently to want to share the first weekend of her career at St. Peter's Hospital with her. She could tolerate Elspeth, but Elspeth's presence would certainly spoil the occasion for her.

For her last night at home, Mitcham took Susan out to dinner at the Falcon restaurant. He had intended to invite Buller and Elspeth to join them there, but Susan had dissuaded him. Susan wanted the occasion to be special, romantic, and this would not be achieved with the presence of her father and the dour Elspeth. For the same reasons, Mitcham had been relieved by her insistence that they dine alone, even though he felt a little awkward that Buller was not able to share his last evening at home with his daughter. Mitcham ordered a glass of champagne each, and then, after they had sat down at the table, told her that he was falling in love with her and that he would find her absence in London unbearable. Dewy eyed, Susan responded that she was in love with him, in such full and unambiguous terms that Mitcham was left in no doubt of her sincerity and the depth of her passion. This was reinforced by her passionate kissing and embrace later in the evening. Mitcham finally deposited her at her home, and, after a lingering kiss, he watched her happily saunter up the drive to the front door, turn and blow him a kiss. The bedroom light went out as she opened the door.

Next morning Mitcham drove to the local florists and ordered and paid for a bouquet of cut flowers to be sent to Susan's new address early the next week. He did not know her room number and said that he would telephone the shop later that day to tell them Susan's room number. He inscribed the accompanying card with the message: 'Darling, Wishing you every success in the coming year. Every second you will be in my thoughts. Dearest love, Graham.' He then drove on to Susan's home where she and her father were just finishing breakfast.

The actual drive to London down the M1 was uneventful. The conversation was not. Susan was excited. She talked enthusiastically about the year ahead, explaining the work routine to Graham.

Shifts called "A" meant that she was on duty. Shifts called "B" meant that she was on call and could not leave the confines of the hospital and the hostel. Normally there would be two consecutive shifts of "A" followed by a "B" shift. Then there would be two days off to recuperate before the shift system repeated itself. She understood that her first six months' tour of duty would be in surgery, followed by a two weeks' holiday. Then the second six months' tour of duty would be in medicine. Having completed both tours successfully she would become a house doctor, hopefully at St. Peter's Hospital. Two years of this and she could then transfer to the GP course. Mitcham had been aware of this programme, as Susan had talked about it in bits and pieces over the previous weeks. But the reality of it all depressed him as he drove along. Would their relationship survive this test? Would, in fact, he really meet her very much? To try to fit her free time in with his office routine and the demands of his practice would be exacting. And if they could not see each other regularly would the relationship fizzle out? Susan, sensing his thoughts, reassured him that whenever she had free days she would come home to spend time with her father and Graham. Perhaps it would work, Mitcham reflected ruefully.

Susan's room in the hostel was an attractive bed sitting room with an en-suite bathroom. Mitcham noted grimly that the bed was only a single bed. 'Sleeping together would be an athletic if uncomfortable occupation,' he thought. Whilst he carried suitcases and boxes containing her possessions from the car to her room, Susan emptied them and arranged them around the room. She carefully perched her portrait of Graham on the top of her bedside cabinet. Finally, standing back to admire the result she turned to Graham and threw her arms around him. "Oh. I love you, Graham!" she exclaimed. And then "Let's go and explore." They set off to explore the hostel, and the public parts of the hospital, and finally the Doctors' mess where they celebrated her arrival with a cup of coffee each. Later they caught the Tube into Covent Garden where Graham took her to Rules restaurant for dinner.

Next day they relieved cramped muscles by a stroll through Green Park, followed by a lunch in the hospital staff canteen. Their day together concluded with an emotional farewell. Mitcham had tears in his eyes as he drove away. Susan suddenly felt deflated.

"What was her room like?" had been Buller's slightly envious enquiry of Graham the following morning at work. Graham described the room, the hostel and what they had done that weekend. Buller's eyebrows shot up when Mitcham told him that they had dined at Rules for that was where he had planned to take Elspeth. Mitcham was always one step ahead of him, he reflected. Still he would learn more about his daughter's activities and news from Graham than if her boyfriend was a stranger, he reassured himself. Even though the relationship posed serious dangers for the practice of Buller & Mitcham if it turned sour, he must look at the bright side he told himself.

Mitcham himself felt worn out as he arrived at work. The weekend had been emotionally draining for him as well as tiring, and he had some difficult work to attend to that morning for which he did not feel mentally equipped. Susan had told him that she would not be able to see him the following weekend as she wanted to reserve it for her father, so that she could give him her undivided attention. Whilst Mitcham had quite understood her reasoning, her wish not to see him had jarred. Was this a sign that

35

his apprehension had foretold?

March 1980

Mitcham need not have worried. The six months passed, quickly for Susan, more slowly for him. A pattern emerged. They met on weekends whenever she was off duty, and occasionally, when the opportunity arose, Graham would spend an evening midweek with her. Almost without fail Susan telephoned Graham each evening, or, if she could not because of work duty, she would leave him a message on his answer phone ending with a declaration of her love for him. Rarely could Graham connect with her on the telephone as she was on duty so much, having to content himself with leaving messages and awaiting her communication. Occasionally Susan came home on a free weekend to stay with her father. Her rota only threw up a free weekend sporadically, and it was rather pointless to go home during the week when her father and Graham were at work all day and there was nothing much for her to do apart from cooking the evening meal for her father, when she could rest in her room at the hostel. For the shifts were exacting, very long and relentlessly tiring, and she needed to rest in her breaks. Much as she needed to see Graham, their activity together was tiring in itself and she needed to conserve her energy for the work ahead.

So, the first six months passed as they each had predicted. Susan threw herself into her new role with a commitment that surprised even herself. She enjoyed the satisfaction of putting her knowledge into practice. Required to attend the operating theatre, she was thrilled at first, and then totally absorbed in studying the techniques applied in the operating theatre. Occasionally she was shown a technique and allowed to perform it herself. Gradually her confidence grew as her inexperience diminished. She witnessed drama as surgeons or anaesthetists struggled to save lives or to correct errors. The first time that she had been allowed to cut open a patient's skin was a nerve-racking experience which painstakingly, and with relief, she performed to the surgeon's satisfaction. As her experience grew so she was allowed to perform more techniques. At times, her monitor would sound and she had to run fast to join the team to assist in saving the life of a patient suffering from a cardiac arrest. Dressed smartly in her white coat, she attended, with the house doctor and registrar, her consultant's ward rounds, answering medical questions directed to her from time to time. This could be embarrassing when she did not know the answer or gave the wrong answer, and received a peremptory grunt from the consultant. But, as her colleagues assured her, this experience happened to everyone. And each evening, whenever she had the opportunity, she would telephone Graham to relay her day's experiences to him and tell him how much she was missing him and to assure him how much she loved him. For she was in love with Graham, and in thrall to her work.

CHAPTER FOUR

As the end of her first tour of duty approached, Graham's thoughts turned to how Susan would like to spend the two weeks of her holiday. "What sort of holiday would you like? A skiing holiday or a beach holiday in the sun somewhere?" Graham asked her one day. "If we can find snow, I would love to go on a skiing holiday" was her immediate reply. Her holiday dates were the last two weeks of March.

"If we go high enough, say the Chamonix valley in France, we should find snow," Graham replied. So, they researched the French and Swiss Alps for suitable snow and accommodation possibilities. After some investigation, they opted for the Chamonix valley in which Graham had skied before.

"I want somewhere quiet and restful in beautiful scenery with good skiing and lovely restaurants," said Susan one evening. "Well, Chamonix is a large, bustling touristy town," replied Mitcham. "And it is set at the foot of magnificent mountain scenery dominated by the towering Mont Blanc. Argentiere, a few miles up the valley is much smaller and you can access the Grands Montets ski field from there, which provides some of the most challenging off-piste skiing in the world. Or there is Les Houches further down the valley, which hosted the first winter Olympic Games. But at the very top of the valley is the Le Tour ski field. I have skied there several times and enjoyed it."

"That sounds perfect to me," enthused Susan. So, they concentrated their research on accommodation in the Chamonix valley. By chance they discovered that a ski holiday firm were offering apartments to rent in the village of Le Tour which were close to the ski lift, and in a telephone call they ascertained that there were several vacant apartments available to rent. So their holiday was booked for two weeks, much to the irritation of her father who had hoped to enjoy her company for at least a few days in that period, and who further realised that he would have to look after his partner's active files during that period, in addition to his own work and worries.

March 1980

They hired a car at Geneva airport, and sped along the autoroute through magnificent mountainous scenery, culminating in the uphill climb via a viaduct from Saint Gervais-les -Bains through into the Chamonix valley. Susan gasped at the sheer majesty of Mont Blanc which dominated the valley. Snow lay around, gradually getting deeper as they ascended.

They sped through Chamonix and then Argentiere, Graham pointing out several restaurants and bars which he had frequented in the past when he had stayed there. A winding road took them up to the village of Le Tour. They parked the car, and stumbled through the snow along narrow lanes bordered by exquisite, ancient wooden chalets, weighed down by heavy drifts of snow, looking for the chalet housing their apartment.

"Bliss!" exclaimed Susan as she gazed down the valley from their balcony. The valley was spectacular in shape, narrow, long and steep sided, dominated on the left by the towering majesty of the Mont Blanc mountain, and on the right by the heights of Brevent. In the distance, she could discern the town of Chamonix, nestled in a haze of grey mist in the bowl of the valley. The long finger of an icy glacier stretched down the mountainside of Mont Blanc, glinting in the afternoon sunlight. Nearer, the slopes were lined by steep sided forests of pine and larch trees, all clad in snow. The representative of the holiday firm had assured them that the snow should still be good for skiing at that time of the year, and certainly there was an abundance of snow everywhere. Three feet or more of snow lay on roof tops, and equal amounts of snow stood on the roofs of abandoned cars giving them a comical appearance. "Just bliss!" she reiterated as her boyfriend joined her, turning towards him and reaching up to devour him with an urgent kiss. "Heavenly," Graham replied when he detached himself from her embrace. "I do hope that you will like it here".

The next day Susan was surprised at how tired and lethargic she felt. It was not just the fatigue from the travelling of the day before, but the accumulation of tiredness and stress of the previous six months. Work at the hospital had been much more demanding than she had anticipated, even though she had been warned to expect it. By now the sky had closed in, and the weather forecast had warned of snow to come. 'I would not mind just staying in and resting today,' she thought. Reading a good novel would be relaxing and most enjoyable. She did not feel energetic enough to ski that day, and in any event only really wanted to do so if the weather was sunny. For all her sporting prowess, she liked good, dry conditions for whatever sport she indulged in.

Graham did not demur when, over breakfast that morning, she mentioned her preference to stay in and rest that day. He, too, felt exhausted from travel and the exigency of work and was content to postpone skiing for a day in order to recover his energy. So, as they munched at their croissants, they planned their day of rest, a routine largely to be spent in bed to be followed by dinner that night at the local Café Blanche.

"Oh, I love you, Graham!" declared Susan, suddenly hugging him to her. They had just enjoyed a delicious Savoyard cheese fondue in the hospitable alpine styled wooden chalet of the Café Blanche, which was situated only a few minutes' walk from their apartment. Responding to her embrace, Graham kissed her passionately as snow began to fall in little

41

flakes around them, glistening in the moonlight. "I love you too," he murmured into her ear. "I really do love you."

The next day, clad in ski clothes and carrying skis and poles, they climbed into a gondola and sped up the mountain side to the snow field of Le Tour, which glistened in the sunshine. Susan proved to be a cautious but competent skier, and Mitcham relaxed as he conducted her around the various pistes before finally arriving, thrilled and exhilarated at the Charamillon restaurant for lunch on the terrace. The dazzling, towering beauty of Mont Blanc lay in front of them, its peak and ranges clearly defined against the blue sky. "Over there," said Graham, stretching his arm in the direction of a mountain slope midway towards Mont Blanc, "lie the Grands Montets ski slopes. We must go there before the holiday ends."

Susan shuddered, knowing that one had to be a very good skier to cope with the challenges of that ski field. She nodded her head affirmatively. Graham was an accomplished skier and she did not want to deny him the thrill of skiing there. She dismissed the challenge from her mind and concentrated on the dramatic scenery that lay before her. The beauty was stunning. She traced the glaciers that sprawled down the mountain slopes to the valley floor beneath. In the shimmering heat of the valley floor she could see Argentiere and further on Chamonix. The Glacier des Bossons seemed to stretch from near the summit of

Mont Blanc down to the fringe of the town, like a tentacle. "If we go to Chamonix one day," said Graham, "we could take the funicular railway up to Montenvers on the side of the Mer de Glace and watch the skiers ski down the glacier. It is an awe-inspiring sight." Susan experienced a slight tremor of anxiety.

"Like connubial bliss," thought Mitcham as he stretched out in bed and gazed lovingly at the sleeping form of Susan. The holiday had passed in an indulgence of excellent skiing, lovely mountain air and scenery, delicious food in alpine restaurants, surpassed only by the luxury of their love-making and being together. "To think that this will end in two days' time and I shall be back at work and Susan will be in London," he shuddered at the thought.

The course of Susan's next tour of duty passed in much the same way as the first tour. Only this time Susan was discovering the intellectual joys of medicine. Less dramatically demanding than surgery, it was equally emotionally draining, particularly in the nursing and care of terminally ill patients. She endured with some suffering the death of the first patient for whom she had, in a supervised way, cared; an elderly lady in her early eighties with cancer of the stomach to whom, in her dying days, she had administered morphine to relieve her pain. The lady's

43

death had affected her more deeply than she had expected. But she knew that it was an aspect of her work that she would have to get used to. This pain was counterbalanced by her exposure to the clinical side of medicine: the diagnosis of illness, the selection of medicine to treat the diagnosis, the constant monitoring of the patient's condition and the timing of the administration of drugs. A very stressful ministry, she concluded, mentally and emotionally demanding.

Mitcham arrived early at her hostel one Friday evening. Susan was not there. He let himself into her room, made himself a cup of tea and settled down into an armchair to await her arrival. After a while the door opened and a tired Susan entered. Her appearance in her white tunic with a stethoscope hanging around her neck surprised him. Mitcham suddenly saw a doctor before him. Although he had appreciated that Susan was a doctor, he had not seen her in uniform with a stethoscope before. It brought it home to him the scale of the responsibility of the duties that his girlfriend was performing. He would indeed have to be careful that he did not demand too much of her time, he thought wisely, if not a little sadly.

September 1980

Mitcham and Susan celebrated the completion of her second tour of duty with a holiday in the Le Sirenuse hotel in Positano on the Amalfi coast in Italy. A fortnight in the sun was what they needed, to be spent sunbathing by the pool, dining in style under the stars, and exploring Amalfi, Sorrento and Capri. When restless they joined excursions to Pompeii and Herculaneum, and marvelled at the ruins and artefacts on display there. The holiday passed only too quickly. Refreshed they returned to their respective homes and careers. Susan had wondered whether Mitcham would propose marriage to her while on holiday, but he had not, although he seemed as much in thrall with her as ever. She had dismissed the thought as too premature, and concentrated instead on the year ahead. Before the holiday, she had applied for a year's contract as a house doctor in the A & E department of St. Peter's Hospital. She had been accepted, much to her delight. Now, at last, she could begin to gain experience in her chosen field. And she had been allowed to keep her room in the hostel, which would make life easier for her.

Mitcham returned to the office refreshed and eager for work. While on holiday he had given some thought as to when he would propose marriage to Susan. He was deeply in love with her, and there had been no doubt in his mind that she was equally in love with him. But she had been so tired when they arrived in Italy that he thought that it was more important that she should rest and refresh, ready for the year ahead. He decided that the opportunity would present itself in the coming year as Susan learned to cope better with the pressures of work, and they could begin to plan their future together.

The firm of Buller & Mitcham continued to expand. An ever-increasing stream of clients were attracted to the firm by its evolving reputation as a modern, competent firm of solicitors. Young solicitors were attracted to the practice, and Buller and Mitcham found no difficulty in recruiting able solicitors. Departments were set up to offer a more specialist service in each discipline. This, in turn, attracted more clients and more profitable work in their wake. Mitcham began to concentrate his efforts on company and commercial work. Buller continued with his mix of probate and conveyancing work: Mitcham had not been able to persuade Buller to concentrate on just one or the other field. As they expanded, they appointed three salaried partners. Partners' meetings, which had been a more casual affair, took on a formal nature, meeting on the first Thursday of every month around the Board Room table to discuss the accounts, and future development of the firm. Mitcham led these meetings, encouraging the new recruits to the partnership to participate in discussions. Buller preferred to sit back and allow his younger colleague to lead the way. After all it was his pension and capital account that their efforts were building up, after all those years of decline. The new salaried partners had proved to be good appointments, and the firm was prospering under their efforts.

Susan felt more confident in her new post. The previous year's training had developed her skills and knowledge, and instilled a quiet authority in her. Now, at last, she would be able to embark on the field of medicine that interested her the most and which would, she hoped, prove to be the linchpin of her career. And, besides being awarded a substantial increment in her salary, she would be entitled to holiday breaks. A slightly more ordered year of activity lay ahead.

CHAPTER FIVE

"How about going to the Lake District for a few days in June?" Mitcham casually asked her. Susan nodded enthusiastically. "That would be wonderful, Graham," she exclaimed. Together they searched through brochures looking for suitable locations and hotels. But the areas that Mitcham had in mind – Windermere and Derwentwater were fully booked – and they had to look further north. They found that The Partridge Inn at Bassenthwaite lake had a room with a double bed and en-suite facilities available, and they reserved that immediately for a week. They could hardly contain their excitement.

June 1981

The drive to the Lake District was uneventful, apart from the traffic jams in the Lakes. Neither of them had been to the Lake District before, so the slow traffic gave them an opportunity to admire the scenery and to familiarise themselves with the topography of the area.

The Partridge Inn had formerly been a coaching inn. Modernised and comfortably furnished, it had a beautiful bar saloon encased in memorable wooden beams and panelling. 'We shall be very happy here,' Mitcham thought.

48

The next day, after a hearty full English breakfast, they walked to the edge of the lake. There was not a cloud in the sky, and the sunlight shimmered on the lake surface. On the other side of the lake rose Skiddaw, a brooding mountain, at 2,500 feet the highest in England. "Let's climb that mountain," Mitcham enthused. "But we do not have climbing boots," protested Susan. "No, but we have walking shoes," responded Mitcham, "They will be sufficient. It does not look too high."

So, savouring the morning sunshine and the still, clear mountain air, they set off along the water's edge in the direction of Skiddaw. Mitcham was excited, for he had plans which he had not shared with Susan. After an hour or so they reached the base of Skiddaw and started the ascent. Mitcham was right. Climbing boots would have been better, but their walking shoes had sufficient grip for the grassy slopes and ensuing dry scree that took them to the summit.

After an hour and a half of steady walking they reached the top, and stood admiring the magnificent views all around. They could see for miles, and excitedly sought to identify landmarks. Deciding that she needed a map, Susan turned and bent over her rucksack, rummaging for the map. On extracting the map, she turned to see that Mitcham had dropped on to his knee and was looking up at her with an excited expression on his face. "What are you doing down there, Graham?" she asked.

"Darling," he replied. "Will you do me the honour of marrying me?" Susan gasped with delight. Simple words, simply and sincerely expressed, promising a commitment for life on his part and hers. "But, of course, Graham. I was wondering when you would pluck up the courage to ask me," she teased, and then flung her arms around him and sobbed as excitement flowed through her. "I love you. I love you and always will. You are the most wonderful man I have ever met, and I promise that I shall try to be the best and most loving and faithful wife you could ever find." Her legs began to give way, and they collapsed laughing and excitedly to the ground. "Oh, my darling," soothed Mitcham. "I cannot wait to be your husband."

They perched together on a big rock, surveying the scene below, talking excitedly about their future together. Tentative plans were discussed. They both realised that, with this simple declaration of love and engagement, they had entered a new, different phase of their relationship, a deeper commitment than only a few minutes before. "When we get back the hotel I must telephone your father to ask his permission to marry you," Mitcham said. "I hope that he does not ask me what my prospects are!" he laughed.

Eventually Mitcham and Susan decided that it was time to descend. Mitcham wanted to complete the circle of the lake which involved going down the opposite slope. On that side of Skiddaw, at the far end of the narrow lake, was, according to the map, 'Mire'. Neither of them fully appreciated what the word 'Mire' described and, in their exhilaration, dismissed it from their minds. They scrambled and slid down the scree strewn mountain side until, with relief, they reached grassland at the bottom. Walking speedily towards the lake's edge they discussed their marriage plans and then sauntered along the shore towards the far end of the lake. They stopped to look back at Skiddaw rising majestically behind them. "To think that we got engaged on that summit," Susan laughed. "We shall have to call it 'our mountain'."

They walked confidently on, chatting non-stop. Suddenly Mitcham, who had been walking lakeside of Susan, felt the ground soften under his footsteps. The softness of the ground did not register with him at first until he realised that his feet were sinking into the ground. "Better move further away from the lake's edge," he warned Susan as he stopped, only to find that his feet had sunk up to his calves. Susan shrieked as she saw what was happening and hurriedly and safely moved on to firmer ground. The subsoil had no stability, no resistance, as Mitcham struggled to raise his right leg out of the mire. 'Oh, why have I not been more careful?' thought Mitcham, realising too late the significance of the word 'Mire' on the map. But he found the mud, slimy and brown, pulling him downwards. 'Christ,' he exclaimed as his legs continued to sink, 'this is going to be the shortest engagement on record!'

Panicking, as Susan screamed for help, he looked

desperately around. No good asking Susan to reach for him, he thought, even though she was standing only two or three yards away from him. She would only sink as well. He spotted a long, stout branch lying at the back of the shore. "Go and get that branch," he yelled, waving his arm in the direction of the branch. The movement made him sink further and he saw in alarm that the mud was now up to his knees. 'This is all going to be over very quickly at this rate,' he panicked. Susan swiftly seized the branch and brought it to where she had been standing. "Now project it, don't throw it, towards me and hold on to the end." Susan obeyed, gingerly protruding the branch towards Mitcham. "Don't drop it, otherwise it will sink too," shouted Mitcham, as his legs sank up to the bottom of his thighs. 'My last chance,' thought Mitcham, 'thank goodness she is athletic and strong. Otherwise I would not have a chance.'

In a sudden lurch, he grabbed hold of the end of the branch. "Now slowly pull me in," he commanded. It worked. Very slowly, with much puffing and panting, Susan reeled Mitcham into the shore. The mud clung to him, but could not restrain his forward movement. As he neared the shore, Mitcham crawled on his stomach on to firmer ground, still grasping the branch in his left hand. Tired, he lay on the firm ground before raising his mud-covered body into a sitting position, whilst Susan sobbed in shock at what had happened. Eventually, recovered from their ordeal, they continued their tour of the lake, making a long detour away from the area marked 'Mire' on the map.

On entering the foyer of The Partridge Inn, the first person whom they met was the Manager, who looked up and down the mud-covered Mitcham in astonishment. Reminding himself that Mitcham was a guest, he greeted him. "Enjoyed your walk, Mr. Mitcham?" before scurrying away as the bracken stench from the mud clinging to Mitcham struck him. Mitcham and Susan quickly strode through the entrance hall and dashed up the staircase to their room.

Immersed in a very hot bath, it took a long time of hard scrubbing before Mitcham was clean again. Reflecting on the vicissitudes of the day, his excitement in proposing marriage to Susan, his happiness and joy that she had accepted, his brush with death in the mire, his fatigue from his strenuous efforts, and his embarrassment in meeting the Manager of the hotel when he arrived at the hotel covered in mud, he suddenly laughed out aloud. Susan, tired and sore from her own exertions, and nursing similar extremes of emotion, queried the cause of his laughter. "But don't you see?" Mitcham exclaimed, "Life is a cabaret, old chum."

"Now I think that I must telephone your father," Mitcham beamed at Susan, "but first I must order a bottle of champagne to be brought up to our room so that we can properly celebrate our engagement." Dressed in clean clothes and feeling relaxed, Mitcham was ready to talk to Buller.

Buller was just about to leave the office and go to 'The Griffin', a nearby pub which had served him lunch nearly every weekday since it had opened for business some years before and to which he often went for a drink after work before returning home. "Buller speaking," he snapped. "Oh, Graham, it is you! Where are you? How is Susan? Are you both all right?" he asked, taken aback that Mitcham had telephoned him at that time of day when on holiday with his daughter. The next question from Graham made him sink back into his office chair. "John, I would like your permission to marry Susan." "Yes, of course," Buller replied with alacrity. "Nothing would give me greater pleasure. It will be wonderful to have you as my son-in-law. It will restore some seniority for me," he added teasingly. They both laughed, even more so when Mitcham explained that he had just asked Susan to marry him on the summit of Skiddaw. "Did she accept your proposal?" enquired Buller. "Oh, yes, of course," was the excited reply. Buller then talked briefly with Susan, congratulating her on her engagement, assuring her that Mitcham was a splendid man and would make a superb husband, and telling her how proud her mother would have been for her. Tears welled up in Susan's eyes as she gazed adoringly at Mitcham.

Buller had steeled himself many months before for such an announcement. As their relationship had developed and matured, he realised the inevitability that one day Mitcham and Susan would marry. He had given a great deal of thought to it, finally concluding that it would be the best arrangement all round. It would bring Mitcham into the family and cement his career with the firm. Buller had always been apprehensive that the lively, ambitious mind of Mitcham might be tempted to leave the firm for better opportunities elsewhere. Marriage to his daughter made this possibility and the consequential breakup of their partnership highly unlikely. 'The best solution all round,' he enthused to himself. 'Almost a cast iron guarantee that Mitcham will spend his career with the firm.'

Mitcham then excitedly telephoned his parents to tell them of his engagement to Susan. Although they had never met Susan, Mitcham had kept them informed of his intentions. They were delighted, and particularly pleased to speak with Susan for the first time, assuring her that their son was very fortunate to have found her. Arrangements were made for them to be introduced to Susan on the young couple's return from the Lake District.

Later that evening, tired but elated, they discussed wedding plans over dinner at the hotel. Tentatively they decided to hold the wedding in June of the following year, timed to follow the conclusion of Susan's career at St. Peter's Hospital.

Susan had never been to York before. She marvelled at the old Roman city walls which encircled the old part of the city, and admired Bootham Gate and Micklegate as they passed by them. From afar she could see the majestic Minster, which dominated the sky line. Mitcham promised that one day he would show Susan around the city. They drove on to Escrick, a pretty, little village some six miles outside York where his parents lived in a small detached bungalow. Mitcham's father had been a headmaster at a noted Grammar school, but was now retired. They were thrilled to meet Susan, and opened a bottle of champagne to celebrate their son's engagement.

Mitcham was their only child, and their love for him was evident to Susan. They did not have the chance to see him often, and they listened attentively to the young couple's wedding plans. "You promise that you will come up for a weekend and spend some time with us, so that we can get to know Susan better," they implored the young couple as they departed for their return south.

Back at the office, at the end of a busy day, Buller convened an impromptu office party to announce the engagement of his daughter to Mitcham. Susan was present, blushing shyly as her father asked everyone to raise their glasses of champagne to toast the young couple. There was a round of applause. Miss Turvey told Susan that in the office she always referred to Mitcham as "my Valentine" which made everyone laugh, and caused Susan to look quizzically at Mitcham. Mitcham in turn told the surprised assembly how it had nearly been the shortest engagement on record. 'I thought that he had more sense than that,' thought Buller.

After the party was over Mitcham took Susan out to dinner at a local Italian restaurant for a farewell dinner. The next day Susan was scheduled to return to work. Later that evening, from his parked car, Mitcham watched Susan saunter happily up the path to her front door, turn and blow him a kiss, and then let herself into the house. At the same time, he noted the upstairs bedroom light turn off. Even though they were now engaged, her father could not relax, Mitcham thought. "Old habits die hard," he murmured to himself.

On the following Saturday, they toured the jewellery shops in Bond Street and the Burlington Arcade, looking for an engagement ring for Susan. Susan had definite ideas on what she wanted in an engagement ring, a sapphire embedded in a white gold ring which was encrusted with small diamonds. Eventually at Bentley & Skinner in Bond Street they found such a ring within Mitcham's budget and bought it. They left the shop, and retraced their steps through the Burlington Arcade into Piccadilly. There they crossed the road and walked to the nearby St. James's Church. Entering the beautiful church, Mitcham ushered Susan into a pew at the back of the nave. Opening the little leather case, he extracted the shining engagement ring and slipped it over Susan's outstretched finger, asking her again, "Will you marry me, darling?" "Yes. Willingly. I love you with all my heart," was her immediate reply. Mitcham gently, reverently kissed her, and for some minutes they sat still holding hands, savouring the significance of the occasion. 'It really is true, not a dream! How lucky I am to be engaged to marry this wonderful man!' thought Susan. Serenely they emerged holding hands into the afternoon sunlight.

CHAPTER SIX

They spent the next few months happily planning
their wedding and honeymoon. Lists of guests were
drawn up, discussed with parents and altered until
agreed. One hundred and twenty guests were the
final number. Mitcham invited Gary, an old college
friend, to be his best man, giving him firm
instructions that his stag party was not to be seedy or
embarrassing. They decided to hold the wedding at
Saint Swithun's Parish Church in Menston, as they
both loved the Church, and his firm occasionally did
little legal tasks for them, albeit for no fee. Mitcham
introduced his smiling fiancée to the vicar, Reverend
Paterson, a rotund man who knew Mitcham well and
was only too happy to assist. A date was set for
Thursday, the 17th of June in the following year, and a
timetable for them to meet and discuss the religious
implications of their vows, the dates of publication of
their banns of marriage, and other matters, was set.
The manager of Menston Hall, an old stone mansion
set in parkland on the edge of the Market Square
which now operated as an upmarket hotel, agreed to
reserve the date for a wedding reception. The happy
couple pored over holiday brochures, looking for a
suitable venue for a honeymoon. They both agreed
that they wanted a quiet, romantic venue, situated in
stunning scenery, in a sunny climate which was not
too hot. After much research, they chose the hotel
Eden au Lac in Montreux on Lake Geneva. This
hotel appeared to meet their criteria in every respect.
The hotel had rooms available overlooking the lake,
and they booked a double room for seven nights. In

the meantime, Susan happily scoured bridal
magazines looking for ideas for her wedding dress.

December 1981

By Christmas plans were well advanced. Susan had
chosen the design of her white wedding dress and the
dresses of her two bridesmaids, both cousins of hers.
But she was not able to see Mitcham over Christmas
as she was on duty at the hospital. A & E
departments are always busy over Christmas, and she
had not been allowed to be off duty. Mitcham had
visited her on the day before Christmas Eve, and
taken her out for a sumptuous dinner at Rules in
Maiden Lane. Later, having returned to her room in
the hostel, they exchanged Christmas presents,
sealing each gift with a kiss before settling down for
the night.

The next day saw Mitcham heading north to York to
spend Christmas with his parents. His last Christmas
with them as a single man, he reflected.

"Where shall we spend New Year's Eve?" Susan had
asked Mitcham some weeks before, having
ascertained that she would be off duty on that day and
New Year's Day. New Year's Eve this year would be
special for them both, marking the end of an exciting
year and heralding an even more exciting and

significant year in their lives. 'Something really special was needed,' thought Mitcham. "Leave it all to me," grinned Mitcham. "I shall have a surprise for you." He was aware that the Savoy Hotel in the Strand in London had a reputation for promoting a lavish New Year's Eve dinner dance. So, next morning he telephoned the Savoy Hotel and reserved a table for two and a double room for the night. He also arranged for a bottle of house champagne in an ice bucket and two champagne flutes to be placed in their room before their arrival. That accomplished, he left a message on Susan's answer phone, assuring her that a New Year's celebration was all arranged and that she would need to wear an evening dress. "Mission accomplished," he murmured to himself happily.

1982

The next year, having completed all arrangements for their wedding, the happy couple turned their thoughts to where they would set up their first home. Susan had secured a GP training course in nearby Leicester City Hospital to start in the September following their wedding, so a home in the vicinity of Menston was the obvious location. Mitcham's flat in Menston, whilst adequate for the short term, was not suitable. So, they decided to sell the flat and to buy a house. Mitcham put his flat up for sale. In the buoyant housing market, a buyer was quickly found for Mitcham's flat. They commenced a thorough search of the local housing market. After much research and house viewings they selected a newly built four bedroomed detached-house with a large garden in Manley Road, which was located in a leafy suburb of Menston. They agreed that initially the house would be bought in Mitcham's sole name, but that once they had married he would put the ownership of the house into their joint names.

'One of the perks of the trade,' thought Mitcham, sitting at his desk, as he contemplated the set of conveyancing papers relating to their house purchase, which had arrived in that day's post at the office. 'At least I shall not be paying someone else to do this for me.'

In early April, they simultaneously completed the sale of the flat and the purchase of their new home. Mitcham picked up the keys to their new house from the Estate Agents' office. That evening Mitcham triumphantly unlocked the front door, and stooped to pick up a thrilled fiancée and carry her, squealing with delight, over the threshold into their new home. "Welcome to our new home, my darling!" he exclaimed.

April 1982

Gary, his best man, picked the hapless Mitcham up at his office later that month. Although Mitcham had been told to take his passport and an overnight case, he knew nothing of what lay in store for him. Gary whisked him away to a chorus of wolf whistles from the office staff who had gathered at the office front door to see him on his way. Buller, watching the scene from behind his office window, scowled. The wedding day was fast approaching and costing him a small fortune, he grimaced.

It was only when they were in Birmingham airport that Mitcham discovered that his destination was Munich. Reunited with ten friends from his past, Mitcham felt a happy relief. He was likely to emerge from the ordeal ahead with his reputation reasonably intact, not in shreds as he had feared.

In the Hofbrauhaus later that evening, the party of boisterous young men, seated at long wooden tables, sang and jostled with one another as they downed litre upon litre of beer from litre pot tankards brought to them by smiling waitresses dressed in Bavarian costumes. Hangovers next day were on order.

But, instead of the lie-in that Mitcham had confidently expected, he was yanked out of bed at 8 o'clock in the morning by his best man and, after washing and dressing himself, unceremoniously shoved into a waiting coach. Inside the coach were his other guests, drowsy or nearly asleep, who gave him a half-hearted cheer as he climbed aboard. He slumped down next to his best man. The coach sped away. The city centre changed into dull suburbs, and transmogrified into countryside, eventually giving way into hilly, then mountainous terrain.

At 10 o'clock precisely the coach stopped on a jetty next to the icy, fast running River Isar. Eleven tired bodies clambered down from the coach, and eyed a massive log raft, which was moored up to the jetty. "After you, Captain," Gary commanded and pushed the limp Mitcham towards the craft. The others followed. They all climbed aboard, and were astonished to find that, in addition to a crew of three swarthy men, was a band of three musicians, and a party of a dozen young men and women. Mounted on the fore deck was a massive barrel of beer. The band struck up, the Captain cast off, and the square sail on the mast was hoisted up. The raft was swept away by the fast running river. As the raft neared the first weir, the Captain ordered the crew to gather in the sail and stow it away. The raft shuddered as it flowed down the long weir, whilst its passengers held on to anything firm that would steady them. With a smack, the raft exited the weir into the fast running current, and the band struck up a rendering of the "Snow Waltz" as the crew thrust long quant poles into the banks of the river to keep the raft in mid-stream. The raft settled down to a fast rhythm, the band to a steady jazz rhythm interspersed with German oompah beer drinking songs, and the Captain ordered that the beer be served. The passengers needed no further prompting. As the sun beat down, and the pace of the river slowed, the raft meandered through pretty countryside, before mooring at lunchtime at an old inn built on the banks of the river. Groggy passengers stumbled off, into the pub's restaurant where they sat down to a hearty Bavarian meal of white sausages and sauerkraut, washed down with beer. Mitcham was euphoric. "What a wonderful stag do!" he shouted to Gary. "What a brilliant idea!"

Later, inebriated, they all struggled back on to the raft, to continue singing, drinking and dancing as the raft glided along the river. By the time the raft entered the outskirts of Munich the barrel was empty. One of the Germans, who had been standing in the stern, wobbled as the raft suddenly lurched, and he fell overboard into the cold, white water. Shrieks and shouts filled the air. "Man overboard!" shouted the Captain rather nonchalantly. Everyone rushed to the side of the raft as the crew threw a lifebelt to the man. Following a wink from Gary, Mitcham suddenly found himself uplifted by his friends, and after a count of "Eins, Zwei, Drei" propelled overboard. The water was icy cold. Mitcham thrashed around, grabbing at something in the water which turned out to be Gary, who had been pushed in after him. They struggled to the river shore and watched the raft disappear out of sight, by now depleted of quite a few passengers who were struggling in the water, the band playing merrily on. Wet through, shivering from the cold, they boarded a crowded autobus heading into the centre of the city.

Much later, after a hot bath and a change of clothes and shoes, Mitcham rejoined his friends at the Hofbrauhaus where they quaffed more beer, albeit at a slower tempo than the night before.

An early start home next day meant that Mitcham was

able to sober up by the time he reached Menston. Thanking Gary for an ingenious stag do, Mitcham reflected that he only wanted to get married once in his lifetime. He could not stomach another stag do.

Susan had planned a hen party involving her two bridesmaids and three very close friends whom she had invited to her wedding. She had decided to take them to Paris for three nights of revelry in the second week of May, some four weeks before her wedding. She set about making the arrangements for what she hoped would be every bit as good a party experience as her fiancé's stag party.

Although Mitcham had sworn his friends at his stag party to secrecy, details had emerged and Susan had been briefed, much to her delight. Regaling her father of what she had learned, she was surprised that her father had not been amused. 'He is getting old!' she shuddered.

Later that evening she confided in Graham her concern about her father. "He depends so much on me for company and comfort," she confessed. "I worry about how he will cope on his own when we marry and set up home together." "But," Mitcham responded, "it will be no different from now. You are away in London for much of the time. I am sure that he has become used to your absence, and is able to manage perfectly well on his own. And, you know, he loves his memberships of Rotary and his Lodge. Besides, he has Elspeth for company. Our marriage might prompt them to tie the knot, or at least to move in together. The last thing that he would want would be for you to be a spinster all your life, just to look after him. And think what joy little grandchildren will bring to him when we have children. That will be priceless!" Susan nodded, a half smile on her face. She knew that Mitcham was right.

Nevertheless, Susan did feel some unease. She loved her father deeply, and did worry about him. She knew that his public persona concealed loneliness and insecurity. He depended on her for love and company, for making a home for him, and she was far from confident that Elspeth would fill that gap adequately.

That night, in bed, reflecting on this dilemma, Susan reappraised her life and her values. Marriage to a wonderful man, one with whom she was deeply in love, would be counterbalanced by separation from her father. She would never live with him again. But she knew that she had her own life to lead, one which promised an exciting marriage to a man whom she desperately loved, a fulfilling medical career and the prospect of being a mother to her own children. She shivered with apprehension at the thought of having her own children. How would she cope? Would she be able to combine a medical career with bringing up children? It was all very exciting, if a little daunting. "I hope that I can make it all work," she questioned herself, not for the first time.

CHAPTER SEVEN

First week of May 1982

"I have decided to take next week off," Buller announced to Mitcham as they locked the office door for the night. "I haven't had a break for a while, and, as you will be away from the office for a week following your wedding, I think it will be a good idea if I take a short break now and fortify myself for the month ahead. Besides Susan is away on her hen party for the latter part of the week. My work load is in good order so you should not encounter any problems. At least nothing that cannot await my return."

"Good idea," responded Mitcham. "What are you going to do?" "Oh. I shall take Elspeth to Salcombe for a few days. We shall stay at the Imperial Hotel where we always go. We like it there. It is very restful." Buller beamed. 'This is a good idea,' thought Mitcham, 'Long overdue.' His partner rarely took a holiday, and, if he did, he never went for more than a week at a time. He had been very tetchy of late, probably uptight over the wedding. 'Perhaps Elspeth has seized the opportunity and is pressing him to marry her,' Mitcham chortled to himself.

Buller was relieved that Mitcham had not raised any objection to his sudden decision to take a week's holiday in the following week. He reasoned that

Mitcham was in no position to object, but it was reassuring none the less that he had not objected. Buller felt tired, in need of a rest. The pressures of the last few weeks had been grinding him down, and he needed a break from them. Susan had told him that he was looking tired, and that he ought to take a break. Perhaps that was why Mitcham had been so amenable – Susan must have been talking to him about her concerns for his health, he ruminated. Elspeth, too, had been concerned about his health, pressing him to go on holiday and calm down. He was fairly sure that that was the reason for her nagging him to take her to Salcombe. Although Elspeth had in the past suggested that they should marry, he had been able to parry that suggestion, saying that he did not wish to do so whilst Susan was living at home. Although the time was fast approaching whereby that would no longer be the case, he thought it unlikely that Elspeth would broach the subject for some time yet. Although he was very fond of Elspeth, appreciating her love and support for him, he was not certain that he wished to commit himself permanently to be her husband. He enjoyed her company, and her companionship on holiday, even her love making on occasion, but marriage to her – no, that was out of the question.

Elspeth was pleased that she had been able to persuade John to take her on holiday to Salcombe. She was very concerned at what she perceived to be his deteriorating wellbeing. He had seemed very tired, edgy and depressed of late, she thought. A week of rest at Salcombe might do him some good, she reasoned. 'And when we return, hopefully, I will be able to persuade him to have a medical check-up. I am sure that there is something wrong with him,' she worried. She wondered whether the cause might be the strain of Susan's impending wedding to Graham, but, she riposted to herself, surely John expected Susan to marry someone sometime, and who could be better than his junior partner, Mitcham? She was certain that that was not the cause of his depression, his withdrawing into himself, and his bad moods. Now was not the time for raising the subject of marriage, she cautioned herself. She was better off in her present arrangement with him. Still a relaxing week at Salcombe would be a nice change for them both.

Saturday 8th May 1982

Buller and Elspeth drove down to Devon. "John is in a better frame of mind than he has been for some time," Elspeth reflected. Buller indeed felt more relaxed, away from the cares of the office for a whole week. He could not believe it. He would be away from the office for a whole week, with nothing to do but to relax and enjoy good food, the sea air and the supportive, loving and occasionally amusing company of Elspeth. For once he felt romantic.

He had no doubt that Elspeth would respond to any overtures that he might make. She had always obliged him in the past, and enjoyed their trysts as much as he did. He smiled to himself. "I am feeling better already," he grunted as he pressed his foot down on the accelerator.

That weekend Mitcham and Susan put together the final touches for their wedding day. They checked and re-checked the details in their wedding plans and honeymoon, and drew up lists of the clothes and accessories that they would need to take with them on honeymoon. 'Nothing is to be left to chance,' Mitcham thought, although they both knew that they could not vouch for the vagaries of the weather. But the forecasts were promising fine weather for early June, so all might be well on that front too, he assured himself.

CHAPTER EIGHT

Monday 10th May 1982

Monday came; Mitcham bounded into the office. Normally the brooding presence of Buller was there. Buller always arrived early to the office in order to open the post and get the office organised for the day's work. Mitcham was a slow riser and preferred to arrive at the office at 8.30 in the morning after the boring matter of opening the post had been dealt with by his partner. But this week Buller would not be there. That in itself relieved the tedium of opening the day's post. Susan had returned to London, and he would not see her again until she returned to her home after her hen party, which he knew was going to be spent in Paris. A quiet, constructive week's work beckoned. "Hello. My Valentine," Miss Turvey beckoned, with a smile on her face. "Did you and Susan enjoy a good weekend?"

Tuesday 11th May 1982

At approximately 11.45 a.m., Miss Turvey knocked on Mitcham's office door and entered. To Mitcham's surprise she was agitated. Mitcham beckoned her to sit down. "I am sorry to interrupt you, Graham, but this is urgent. Two of Mr. Buller's clients, a Miss Rudd and a Miss Dixon, telephoned me this morning. They were quite angry because they had not received the sale monies from the sale of their house. I

72

explained to them that Mr. Buller was on holiday for a week, but that I would look into the matter and telephone them back. Well!" Miss Turvey paused, and took a deep breath. "I have searched all through Mr Buller's office looking for their file and everywhere else that I can think of, but I have not been able to find it. I have looked at their account on the computer, and this shows that the proceeds of sale were £37,000, that the sale was completed last month on the 18th April and that the estate agents' fees had been paid and that the sum of £35,000 had been paid to the Assurance Bank on the 18th April. I thought that, before I telephone our clients, I ought to bring this to your attention."

Mitcham listened to this grimly. His first thought was that he knew that Buller's personal bank account was with the Assurance Bank. Had Buller put the money into his own account? But Buller would not do a thing like that. Quite out of character. It was more likely that the clients banked with Assurance Bank, and that there had been a posting error by the Bank, or perhaps his firm had made a mistake when inputting the details of the transaction in the clients' ledger. This was always his fear with computerised accounts, he reflected. "Do you know which Bank Miss Rudd and Miss Dixon bank with?" he asked Miss Turvey. Miss Turvey replied that she had not thought to ask them that. She had not been able to find the file, so she was not able to say.

Mitcham gazed at Miss Turvey. He felt distinctly uneasy, and it was clear from Miss Turvey's countenance that she shared the same feeling. "I think that it would be sensible if you carried on looking for the file. It must be in the office somewhere." Miss Turvey looked uncertain. "What do I say to the clients if they ring me?" Miss Turvey asked. "Just say that the matter is being investigated by me and that I will telephone them as soon as I have completed my investigation." Mitcham hoped that this ploy would bring him some breathing space to find out what had happened to the money and to rectify the position.

As Miss Turvey left the room, Mitcham telephoned his secretary to ask her to bring to him the file on personal data that all clients had to complete before giving instructions to the firm. Duly produced, this revealed that Miss Rudd and Miss Dixon did not bank with the Assurance Bank.

"Damn," thought Mitcham, "I do not like the look of this." Mitcham left his room and slowly climbed the stairs to the next floor where the accounts department was situated. In there he found Rose, the accounts clerk, stationed in front of her computer, busily inputting information. "Rose, can you please stop doing what you are doing, and access the client account of Miss Rudd and Miss Dixon." Mitcham tried to smile in order to cover his unease. Rose did as she was asked. Mitcham scrutinised the account. It clearly showed that on the 16th April a cheque for £35,000 had been drawn on the account and made payable to the Assurance Bank. The cheque had been cleared for payment on the 21st April.

"Rose. Can you, please, telephone our Bank and ask them into which branch of the Assurance Bank that sum had been paid?" Mitcham leaned against the wall as Rose dutifully made the enquiry. "The Bank have given me the sort code of the payee Bank," Rose reported. "Can you now ring the Menston branch of the Assurance Bank and ask them whether that number is their sort code." Rose did as she was directed, and a few minutes later was able to confirm that the sort code in question was the sort code of the Menston branch of the Assurance Bank. Mitcham felt alarm. "Please ask them into whose account that cheque of £35,000 had been paid on their receipt of it." Rose did as she was directed, but then frowned. "The Bank refuse to divulge that information," she said. "They say that to do so would constitute a breach of customer confidentiality." Mitcham cursed quietly.

Mitcham returned to his room, closed the door and strode to his office telephone. He pressed the key pad and selected the telephone number of his firm's Bank. "Can you please put me through to the Manager?" he asked. "No, this is private. Just tell him that it is Mr. Mitcham calling him from Buller & Mitcham, the solicitors, and that the matter is extremely urgent."

"Graham, how nice to hear from you. How can I help you?" was the languid answer from Mr. Westlake, the manager of the Menston branch of the Reform Bank, a few seconds later. "James, I am trying to find out into whose account a cheque drawn by my firm for

£35,000 on the 16th April has been credited. I have established that it has been paid into the Menston branch of the Assurance Bank, but they are refusing to tell me the name of that account on the grounds of customer confidentiality. I quite understand that, but I need to know whether the money has been paid to the correct payee. I suspect that it has not. I wondered whether you could have a word with your opposite number at the Assurance Bank and establish the name of the account for me." "Hmm, I will see what I can do," Westlake replied. "I will ring you back shortly." "Thanks, James." Mitcham replaced the handset,

Mitcham paced up and down his room, deep in thought. Would Westlake be able to discover the identity of the account name for him or would the rules of customer confidentiality and Banking Regulations prevent him from doing so? If so, what should his next step be? He was just about to pick up his file containing notes of advice on what to do if a Solicitor suspects a case of money laundering when the telephone rang. "Mr. Westlake for you, Mr Mitcham," said the telephone receptionist. "Hi Graham. The name of the account is Mr John Buller," said Westlake breathlessly, adding "Is anything wrong?" Mitcham froze. "I think that a mistake may have been made," answered Mitcham. "I will contact you when I have been able to verify the position. Unfortunately, my partner is on holiday. I will be in touch. And, by the way, thank you for getting that information for me."

Mitcham sat back in his chair, his mind racing over various scenarios. Could it be a posting error by the Assurance Bank? Had his partner innocently broken Solicitors' Accounts Rules and unintentionally paid the money into his own private Bank account, believing that he was paying it into his clients' Bank account? Or was this a deliberate misuse of clients' money? What steps should he be taking? Should he be reporting the problem to the Law Society? If he was wrong, if he had not investigated the matter thoroughly before drawing the conclusion that his partner had misused clients' money, then the fallout with John would be immense. His partner would never be able to trust or rely on him again. It would inevitably lead to a dissolution of their partnership.

And what would the repercussions be on his intended marriage to Susan, only a couple of weeks away? Mitcham shuddered. It was too heart breaking to contemplate. A wedding in those circumstance: Buller handing his daughter's hand to him in marriage, knowing that Mitcham had just falsely accused him of stealing clients' monies, and reported him to the authorities, would be impossible. Should he telephone John and ask him outright? The damage would be the same. Would it be any better to telephone John and just make tentative enquiries about what he had done in case there was another answer. But if John was misusing clients' money, he would presumably lie or lay a false trail and Mitcham would be none the wiser. Indeed, if he fell for that, then the authorities might conclude that Mitcham was colluding with Buller, and put his own career at risk.

Besides he had two angry clients demanding their money, and he was duty bound by law to pay it to them immediately, without procrastination. Mitcham groaned. And did the firm have £35,000 in its office account to cover the amount owed to the clients? He was certain that it did not. Where was he going to get that amount from? Adrenalin and nervous tension swept through him. He felt sick. It dawned on him that, before he challenged John, he had to know more about the facts and the circumstances surrounding the transaction. He had to be certain of the facts, he had to have no doubt that that he was pursuing the right course. Far too much was at stake, but he had to act quickly.

He rose from his chair, tension preventing him from sitting any longer. He paced up and down the room, gnawing at his thumb. Then he decided on his immediate course of action. He had to make further enquiries, not make hasty decisions whose consequences may come to haunt him.

He pressed the intercom. "Howard. Can you come straight down to my room, please? It is urgent." "But Graham I am in the middle of a reconciliation," was the exasperated reply. "Put it on hold, Howard, this is very urgent."

Howard Chambers was not a man to be trifled with. Acerbic, with a quick temper when aroused, he had headed the accounts department of the firm for over twenty years. Nothing had gone wrong on his watch. He was an indefatigable worker, used to working at high speed and under considerable pressure when business was booming and money transactions were flooding through the accounts department. "Postings of money through the accounts had to be done accurately and at once," he emphasized repeatedly to his assistant, Rose. Nothing passed by him.

A few minutes later there was a knock on Mitcham's door. "You wanted me?" Chambers grumpily enquired. Mitcham beckoned him in, asking him to close the door and motioned him to a chair. Mitcham gazed warily at his accounts manager. Although he had prepared his opening words, he was now uncertain. Chambers had known and worked for Buller longer than for Mitcham and was always very loyal to him. What would his reaction be?

Taking a deep breath, Mitcham began. "A problem has cropped up, Howard. You know that earlier this morning I asked Rose to trace the trail of a cheque on clients' account which John had requisitioned on the 16th April?"

Chambers nodded. He had been present in the accounts room when Mitcham had asked Rose to do this, and had wondered what it was all about. But Rose had known nothing more when he asked her about it, after Mitcham had left the room. He was also aware that Miss Turvey had been looking for that particular file and had not been able to find it. He winced when Mitcham told him that he had asked the firm's Bank manager, Mr. Westlake, to find out from the manager of the Assurance Bank the name of the account into which the money had been paid and had been told that the money had been paid into the private Bank account of John Buller.

"But that is a clear breach of Solicitors' Accounts Rules," he protested. "John would not do a thing like that. You know he would not!" He sat back into his chair and looked critically at Mitcham. "What are you going to do?"

"Before I make any allegations, Howard, I want to be certain of the facts. To raise a cheque on clients' account, a cheque requisition has to be drawn. Can you please find that for me? I want to know what it says, who completed it, and who signed it. Miss Turvey may have told you that we cannot find the clients' file, which is a thorough nuisance. Without it I cannot check what sum is actually owing to our clients. I want to know who took the cheque to the Assurance Bank. Was it John, or a member of this firm? Was there a covering letter, and to whom at the Assurance Bank was it addressed? I need to know this information immediately, but I do not want anyone in the firm to know of my concerns. So, can you, please, be very discreet in how you proceed, allay any questions that employees may ask of you as best you can, and report back to me as soon as you can. If I am engaged with a client, please interrupt me." Howard sprang from his chair, and made for the door. "Utmost discretion, Howard," Mitcham warned him.

Howard's head was in a spin. In all the years that he

had worked for this firm this was the first unsavoury circumstance that had involved him and his department. And he could see disaster looming.

The weather was fine in Salcombe. Buller and Elspeth had enjoyed two lovely days relaxing on sunbeds on the hotel terrace, which overlooked the estuary of Salcombe Bay. Sunny days had given way to cocktails at 6 pm., followed by a delicious dinner 'a deux', washed down with copious amounts of red wine. "If only life could always be like this!" he sighed. Elspeth noticed his sigh, and reassuringly stretched out her hand to caress his. 'I hope that he is happy,' she thought to herself. 'He has been working too hard for his own good,' she reflected. She had never entirely approved of Mitcham's appointment as a partner to the firm. His vigour and ambition had certainly expanded the firm and raised John's stature within the community, and increased his income substantially, but it had involved him in considerable extra work and worry. She was not at all sure that it was all worth it. And then Mitcham's forthcoming marriage to Susan, how was that going to impact on John and herself? Already they had worked hard with Susan in making arrangements for the wedding, which was clearly going to cost John a lot of money. Although she knew that he could afford and wanted to give Susan a lavish wedding, she knew that it was causing him extra stress. 'I hope that he can cope with it all,' she reflected. Certainly, he had looked very tired and drawn of late.

Mitcham was talking to Susan on the telephone when Howard knocked on his office door and entered. He looked agitated. Mitcham anxiously motioned him to take a seat. Susan had telephoned him out of the blue to discuss wedding details. Mitcham had engaged as best he could in discussing such items but his mind was elsewhere. 'Rather distracted' was Susan's description of Graham as they ended their telephone conversation, and Graham was free to listen to Howard's report.

Howard first produced the requisition slip. Mitcham studied this carefully. A printed form which required essential details to be written in. The hand writing was unmistakeable. It was clearly in Buller's handwriting, which was spindly but precise. It instructed the accounts department to draw a cheque on the Rudd and Dixon client account for £35,000 in favour of the Assurance Bank. It was dated the 16th April and signed 'J. Buller.' It did not state the account number or name of the payee.

"Hmm," thought Mitcham. "Who signed the cheque?" he asked. Howard hesitated. "I asked Rose that question," he said, "and she told me that Mr Buller had signed the cheque, put it in an envelope, and had instructed her to take it herself to the Assurance Bank and to ask to see their Mrs Green, and to hand it to her and to no one else." Rose had immediately complied with that instruction and duly presented the envelope to Mrs. Green.

82

Howard continued, "After hearing Rose's report, I found a quiet room and telephoned Mrs. Green of the Assurance Bank. I told her that I was making enquiries to help me conduct an audit trail of this particular cheque at the behest of Mr Mitcham and I understood that Rose had delivered a cheque for £35,000 to Mrs Green on the 16th April. Mrs Green said that she was not authorised to answer my question and so put me through to her superior, Mrs Warner. Mrs Warner knew about this cheque and was authorised to answer any enquiries concerning it made by Buller & Mitcham. She confirmed that Mrs Green had received an envelope containing a handwritten note and a cheque for £35,000 drawn by Buller & Mitcham in favour of the Assurance Bank. The handwritten note was signed by a Mr John Buller and directed the Bank to pay the cheque into his private account with the Bank. This the Bank did, and the cheque cleared on presentation. I then asked the Bank to confirm that the sum of £35,000 was still in Mr. Buller's account but Mrs Warner declined to answer this question on the grounds of customer confidentiality. She said that the Bank would need a letter of authority signed by Mr Buller authorising them to disclose his private account to Buller & Mitcham before they could divulge such details."

"Thank you, Howard, you have done very well," Mitcham said, wearily, sinking into his chair. "I do hope that you do not think that my department has done anything wrong?" Howard asked anxiously. "Oh no," Mitcham assured him. Whatever office procedure needed tightening up, now was not the time to discuss it. He needed Howard on his side, and an unsure Howard would be even more anxious to assist him.

"What do we do now?" asked Howard. Mitcham did not answer at first. He considered all the options again, asking himself if there was any point that he had overlooked. He could not think of anything. With an air of resignation, he announced that the time had come to talk to John Buller, holiday or no holiday. "I think that it would be sensible if you stayed and listened to the conversation, Howard."

His heart sinking, Mitcham dialled the telephone number of the Imperial Hotel at Salcombe and asked the receptionist to put him through to Mr John Buller. The receiver was lifted. "Buller speaking." Buller's voice was loud, emphatic and confident. "Hi, John. Graham here. I am sorry to disturb you on holiday, but a problem has cropped up which needs dealing with immediately. By the way, are you and Elspeth enjoying a good time? Oh, good. I have Howard here, I am going to put the phone on loudspeaker. Now what has happened, John, is that Miss Rudd and Miss Dixon telephoned the office this morning demanding payment of their money, some £35,000."

He sensed his partner wilting at the other end of the phone. "We cannot find their file, so we do not know what they are owed. We have looked at their account and it shows that on the 16th April the sum of £35,000 was drawn out of their client account and paid into the Assurance Bank. We have made enquiries of the

84

Assurance Bank, and they say that the money has been paid, on your express written instructions, into your private account at the Bank." Buller interjected, "Oh! That's all right, Graham, I will sort it out when I return to the office on Monday." "But that won't do, John," Mitcham responded emphatically. "This is a clear breach of Solicitors' Accounts Rules, and the Rules require that we make good the breach immediately. Besides I have Miss Rudd and Miss Dixon demanding their money. This cannot wait until next Monday. Can you, please, come back immediately and sort it out."

"That is quite out of the question, Graham," Buller breathed heavily. "I am committed to stay here until Sunday. I will sort it out on Monday when I return to the office." Buller replaced the receiver.

Mitcham was taken aback by his partner's insouciance. "What the hell do we do now?" he muttered, turning to look at an exasperated Howard. "Howard, can you please let me know how much clear funds we have on office account, that is after deducting issued cheques." Howard rose slowly to his feet. "It will not be enough to pay £35,000," he announced gloomily.

Mitcham was in a quandary. His duty was clear. Under Solicitors' Accounts Rules he had to restore the client account of Miss Rudd and Miss Dixon with the sum of £35,000 at once by paying into the client Bank account the sum of £35,000. But from where could he raise that sum quickly? And he also had to pay to

Miss Rudd and Miss Dixon the monies due to them.
But without the file it was impossible to say how
much was due to them. It could be the sum of
£35,000, or much less if there were mortgages to be
paid off. It would be irresponsible, let alone
unprofessional, to ask them how much they thought
was due to them. But what was he to tell them? He
reached for a file containing his own private Bank
account and looked at his own private Bank
statement. A healthy credit balance of £5,000 was a
help, but no more. He sighed. "Heaven knows what
Susan will make of all this," he wondered.

A knock on the door signalled the return of Howard.
"The net balance on office account is £12,000," he
declared. "Hmm. £17,000 I can raise. £18,000
short," Mitcham muttered darkly.

Buller had been alarmed by the telephone call from
Mitcham. He had just enjoyed a lunch with Elspeth
on the terrace, and was on a sunbed in a state of
relaxed doziness when a waiter had disturbed him, to
summon him to the telephone in the hotel lobby.
Mitcham had telephoned. "Damn," he mouthed,
"damn, damn, damn!" He looked at the prostrate
figure of Elspeth, slumped over the adjoining sunbed.
Fortunately, she appeared to be asleep. 'I hope that
she had not been disturbed,' he thought, before
reassuring himself that this was most unlikely. 'Blast
Miss Rudd and Miss Dixon!' He had misjudged
them. He had thought that they would be patient.

They knew that he was about to go on holiday. He had assured them that he would endeavour to get their money to them before he left for his holiday, but that his ability to do so would depend on all monies being cleared before he left. They, the old dears, had seemed content with this assurance. He could not believe that they would be pressing for payment so soon. Surely, they could wait until next Monday? And what about Mitcham, what did he suspect? What would he do? Mitcham was a young, forthright solicitor, who would feel obliged to follow Solicitors' Accounts rules to the letter. But it would not be easy for him to report the breach to the Law Society. Thank God for his imminent wedding to Susan!

But he felt sick in the stomach at the revelation of his breach and the speed at which it had unravelled. Would it be wise to break his holiday and return to the office and sort out the problem before matters deteriorated any further? He looked down again at the supine figure of Elspeth. 'If I did, what would I tell her?' he pondered nervously. It would spoil their holiday. Elspeth was the type who would want to know the detail of why it was so urgent for him to return to the office. 'What should I tell her?' He felt alarm. After a long reflection on the options available to him, he decided to play it long. 'Bluff it out,' he told himself. 'Be a man, not a wimp.' He settled back into his sunbed, and tried to relax.

He did not relax for long. The waiter returned to

report that Buller was wanted on the telephone, his urgent voice making Elspeth stir. With an air of exasperation Buller stomped off to the telephone kiosk in the lobby. "Oh, Graham! What now?" he stormed crossly. "John, the Solicitors' Accounts Rules oblige us to restore client account at once," Mitcham demanded. "Can you please telephone your Bank and arrange for the sum of £35,000 to be transferred to the firm's client account immediately. With any luck, the money could be in our client account this afternoon." "I will see what I can do, Graham. Leave it with me," was the confident reply. "Can you ring me when you have spoken to the Bank?" demanded Mitcham. "Yes, of course, Graham," was the assured reply. Confident and assured may have been his demeanour, but Buller felt sick. He had bought himself a little time, a breathing space, but no more. He knew that Mitcham would not leave the matter alone. Damn him!

It was 4 o'clock. Buller had not telephoned him. Mitcham had seen two sets of clients in the meantime and dictated a few letters, but his heart was not in it. He had not believed Buller when Buller had so speedily promised to telephone his Bank and arrange for the transfer of the money, but he thought that he ought to give him the chance to do so. Mitcham picked up his telephone and dialled the Imperial Hotel at Salcombe. He asked the receptionist, who answered it, to put him through to Mr. Buller. "I have just seen Mr and Mrs Buller take the lift to their floor," the receptionist answered brightly. "I will put you through to their room."

"Buller speaking," the familiar voice of his partner answered. "John, Graham here, did you have any luck with the Bank?" Mitcham asked desperately. "No, Graham. I tried but I could not get hold of Mrs Warner to give her the instruction. I will try again tomorrow morning. In the meantime, I suggest that you explain to Miss Rudd and Miss Dixon that I am on holiday this week, but will sort the matter out on my return to the office on Monday. I am sure that they will understand." "But John..." Mitcham started. "Now I have got to go, Graham. I will contact the Bank tomorrow. Goodbye." With that, Buller hung up. 'I should be able to stall this until Monday,' he assured himself.

The line went dead, leaving Mitcham in strangulated mid-sentence. "'That is no help to me,' agitated Mitcham. 'I had better have words with Miss Rudd and Miss Dixon, and then set about trying to raise £18,000.'

Miss Rudd answered Mitcham's call. "It is good of you to ring, Mr Mitcham," she said, and settled down to hear Mr Mitcham's explanation. "I am in a difficulty, Miss Rudd, as we cannot find your file. I suspect that Mr Buller has it in his briefcase as we have searched the office thoroughly for it and have not been able to find it. Without it I cannot make any arrangements to issue a cheque to you and Miss Dixon, because I do not know what the final figure should be." "We are expecting about £35,000," Miss Rudd responded brightly. "Yes, but under Solicitors' Accounts Rules we have to be accurate in determining what is due to you. I have been in contact with Mr. Buller, who assures me that he will deal with the matter on Monday when he returns to the office. I will see that he does," Mitcham assured her. "Hmm. Well you have done all that you can, Mr Mitcham. Miss Dixon and I will just have to be patient." "Thank you, Miss Rudd." Mitcham replaced the telephone.

Next, he telephoned the firm's Bank and asked to speak to Mr. Westlake. "James, would it be possible, please, to arrange a bridging loan to the firm of £20,000 for a few days, say a week. I would expect to be able to pay it back by then," Mitcham asked. "How quickly do you want it?" was the reply. "I will have to refer your request to my Regional Manager. I will see what I can do."

An hour later Westlake telephoned Mitcham. "The Bank have agreed to your request, Graham, provided that you and Mr Buller sign a letter of undertaking to repay the money to the Bank within seven days. I shall have to get you and Mr. Buller to sign some papers first. Can you both come around to my office tomorrow morning? It is too late to arrange anything for today." Mitcham explained that Buller was on holiday, and it was agreed that Mitcham's signature alone would suffice. 'Hopefully that is one problem solved,' sighed Mitcham.

Next, he transferred £5,000 from his own private bank account into the firm's office account. "I can see that I shall be living off my credit cards," he observed grimly.

Howard was relieved when, at close of business, he met Mitcham in his office and learned of the arrangements that Mitcham had made. "We shall have to defer making payment of office bills for a while," remarked Mitcham. "Can you, please, do a check of the firm's direct debits and standing orders and let me have a list of them and dates for payment. We may have to stop payment of some of these." "What about the other three partners?" Howard asked, "Shouldn't they be told of what is happening?" "Yes, I have already been thinking about that," was the stiff reply. "I want to convene a partners' meeting tomorrow morning, if possible at 9.30 a.m. I want you to be present. I will arrange that now."

Back at his house, Mitcham poured himself a glass of whisky. After a traumatic day like that he needed a stiff drink, and he needed time to collect his thoughts. He seemed to have made arrangements to cover the shortfall on clients' account, Miss Rudd and Miss Dixon had appeared to be prepared to give his firm an extension of time until Monday to pay them their money. He fervently hoped that they would not resort to another firm of solicitors to complain about the delay. That could be embarrassing. The firm's Bank had been very good in agreeing a bridging loan without asking any awkward questions. Not all Banks would be so obliging, he thought ruefully. Hopefully Buller would be able to transfer the £35,000 from his private Bank account into the firm's Client Bank account tomorrow, or at least by Monday. If he could not, then the firm would be in a financial mess. He shuddered. And what was the position of the Assurance Bank? They must have realised that John had paid a client account cheque into his private Bank account, they must have known that this was a breach of Solicitors' Accounts Rules, they must have known that he could not lawfully do this. Surely, they must be accountable for the firm's loss of £35,000? They must be liable under a resulting trust. His head was spinning with these thoughts, when the telephone rang.

"Graham, are you all right?" breathed Susan, "You sounded very distracted today when I telephoned you." "Oh, Susan, thank God it is you. I have had a terrible day." "Are you all right, darling?" Susan repeated her question anxiously. "What has gone wrong? Is there anything that I can do to help you? I am in London, so I cannot give you a massage," she giggled. "No, I am afraid that I cannot talk about it," said Mitcham. "Just a client matter which has gone pear shaped. It will sort itself out in due course, but it has given me a lot of worry today." 'Not half!' he thought ruefully as they turned the conversation on to happier matters – their wedding and the details of her hen party scheduled to start the next day and end on

Saturday. After concluding their conversation and wishing each other sweet dreams and Susan a hen party to remember, Mitcham wondered for how long he would be able to keep the dramatic news from Susan. He knew that he was duty bound to report the facts to the Law Society, that there would be an investigation, and that, in all probability, Buller would be suspended from practice. In any event, he may have to dissolve the partnership himself, perhaps tomorrow?

And what would be the impact of this on their forthcoming marriage? Indeed, would there be a wedding? Thank the Lord that she would be out of the country for the remainder of the week, enjoying herself. He felt sick. A rump steak and a pint of beer were sorely needed, he decided.

Susan replaced the telephone in its cradle. She felt concerned. Graham seemed tired and edgy on the telephone. Although he had said all the right things, she felt that his mind was elsewhere. 'I hope that he is not getting cold feet about marrying me,' she worried to herself, before dismissing the thought. They were so much in love with each other, it was unthinkable that Graham would be having second thoughts about her. 'No, it must be an office or client problem,' she assured herself. It was a pity that her father was on holiday, because he might know what the problem was, and reassure her that it was nothing to do with her or the wedding. 'Perhaps I am worrying myself too much, perhaps it is just a case of pre-wedding nerves.' With that thought she poured herself a small measure of whisky, and settled down to packing her suitcase in readiness for her hen party the next day.

Despite enjoying a rump steak and two pints of bitter at his local pub, the Stag, Mitcham could not relax. Too many thoughts, too many worries crowded his mind. He went to bed early after telephoning Susan to wish her sweet dreams and to tell her how much he loved her, and was missing her. Her response was equally loving and enthusiastic. 'For how much longer?' he asked himself. Would she still love him when the whole wretched story was revealed to her, and her father was suspended from practice and the firm? That would really test the strength of her love for him! And would her father be prepared to give her hand in marriage to Graham, indeed to attend the wedding, let alone to make the father's speech at the wedding whilst all this trauma was unfurling? That surely was asking too much of him. Could he properly delay reporting Buller to the Law Society and delay dissolving the partnership until after the wedding? No, that would not work. The result would be much the same with the addition that he would have proved himself deceitful to Susan and her father. Besides there were the other three partners to consider. He would be playing fire with their careers. In any case, it would be impossible to keep the affair quiet within the office. Howard, Rose and Miss

Turvey already knew most of the details, and the remainder of the office staff knew that there was a missing file and that there was a problem concerning it. And what if Buller was not good for £35,000, what then? At the very least Mitcham needed cover for £20,000. What if Buller could not provide even that sum? Insoluble questions chased one another, revolving through his mind. But sleep failed to come to his aid. Instead he tossed and turned in bed, the nervous pain in his stomach unquenchable.

CHAPTER NINE

Wednesday 12th May 1982

Mitcham arose early the next morning. The bedside clock informed him that it was 7 am. He knew that Susan would be at the airport at Heathrow with her friends, assembled for their flight to Paris at 7.30 am. He could picture their excitement, and envied their escape from reality.

By 8 o'clock Mitcham was at the office, opening the post and thinking furiously about his next steps forward. He was not looking forward to the partners' meeting arranged for 9.30 am. Exactly how was he going to present this? What questions would they ask that he had not already anticipated? What pressures would they exert on him to take steps that he did not want to take, or take at the speed that they required? The best that he could hope for was that they would be sympathetic and cooperative, and maybe suggest better courses of action than he had considered.

At 10.30 am. French time, Susan and her entourage were happily breakfasting on croissants and coffee in a buffet at Charles de Gaulle airport. Confidences were exchanged, legs pulled, stories told; girls giggled and laughed, drawing curious glances from other customers sitting at nearby tables. Paris beckoned.

At 9.30am. Buller stifled a yawn. Seated in the breakfast room, opposite Elspeth who was gazing out to sea, he felt wretched. Beset with worry and tension, he had not been able to sleep the previous night. He had racked his brain all night to find a solution to the terrible predicament that he feared was about to engulf him. Although he had intimated to Mitcham, he was sure that it was only an intimation not a promise nor an undertaking, born of a need to buy himself some time, that he would telephone his Bank and instruct them to transfer by telegraphic transfer the sum of £35,000 out of his private account into the firm's client Bank account, he had not done so. He knew that there was not enough money in his account to enable him to do so. Oh, why could it not all wait until Monday when he would be back at the office to sort it all out? His impulse was to drive straight back to Menston in order to take command of events, but he knew that Elspeth would strongly object to their holiday being curtailed. For, once back at the office, he would have to stay there; he could not just sort the problem out, leave the office and resume his holiday. And, if he were to propose doing that, what explanation would he have to give to Elspeth? It would have to sound both plausible and compelling. And then he would have to give the same explanation to Susan, who was not easy to fob off. She would fish or ferret the truth out of him. And what then? There was no need to accelerate a problem that might not materialise. Besides what would his partners and staff make of it all? How far had the story spread through the office? There was the missing file. Would Mitcham keep his misgivings

97

to himself? Did Howard know? Yes, he must do. And where was he going to find the shortfall from? He would need to borrow, but how much? Without having files to hand he could not estimate how much he would need to borrow. Would his Bank lend to him? Oh, why hadn't he borrowed in the first place? Oh, what a mess! Perhaps he might buy himself some time by sending a cheque to the office. By the time it had failed to clear it would be Monday and he would be back at the office and able to sort things out.

The waitress brought their cooked English breakfasts to their table. Normally his eyes would light up in relish. But Elspeth noted that he gazed at his plate absent-mindedly. 'Obviously his thoughts were elsewhere'. And he looked tired. He toyed with his food. 'Oh dear,' she thought. 'Something is obviously troubling him.' She had been present the previous day when Mitcham had telephoned him, and had noted his nervous reaction and pained expression. His mood had changed since then. He had withdrawn into himself, and become moody. Clearly whatever was troubling him was the result of that phone call. Thankfully it was not her. Nothing to do with her, which was a relief. In fact, he may need her more now than ever. She contented herself with this thought, even though the forecast for the remaining days of their holiday appeared at best to be gloomy. Perhaps the visit to Exeter Races planned for tomorrow would distract him from his mood, she hoped.

There was a sense of tension in the air as the partners and Howard assembled in the Board Room at 9.30 am. Partners' meetings normally took place on the first Thursday of each calendar month after lunch, and were always presided over by Buller. And there was always an agenda with supporting papers and an abridged set of accounts for the previous month's trading with year to date. But this was different. There were no accounts, no agenda, and no Mr. Buller. What was this all about? The three young salaried partners had heard that Miss Turvey had not been able to find one of Buller's files, but, although a rare occurrence, this did occasionally happen and the file would in due course reappear, having been misfiled. Not a matter for an urgent partners' meeting.

Ushering them all to take a seat around the Board Room table, Mitcham cleared his throat. "I know that there is not a written agenda for this morning's meeting, but I have asked Howard to take notes of what is said and any decisions made. First, I want to announce a pay rise of 10 per cent for each of you, including Howard, to take effect from the beginning of this month. You may be surprised that it is announced today, but, in view of what you are all going to learn and have to do in the coming weeks, you will earn it." Mitcham glanced at his four colleagues.

Howard looked pleased, although, Mitcham thought, he looked rather tired. He too had probably endured a sleepless night. The three young partners looked excited and delighted at their sudden and unexpected pay rise. Amanda Thompson, the probate and trust partner, looked at her colleagues facing her. What did Mitcham mean when he said 'in view of what you are all going to learn and have to do in the coming weeks you will earn it'? she wondered. The same thought had occurred to Stephen Jones, the young litigation partner.

"Thank you very much for the pay increase, Graham, but what do you mean by the last statement?" he enquired. "All in good time," responded Mitcham, hoping that he sounded calm and assured. "Now, Howard, perhaps you could give us the up to date financial position on office account." "Just office account?" asked Howard. "Not client Bank account?" "No, just the office Bank account," replied Mitcham, "I want the partners to be aware of the firm's financial position before we move on to the main topic on the agenda." Howard cleared his throat. "As at close of business yesterday the firm had a clear balance on office account of £12,000."

"Thanks, Howard, and is it correct that Mr Buller is scheduled to return from holiday next Monday?" "Yes," replied Howard. The three salaried partners stiffened and looked enquiringly at one another across the table. This was the first mention of Mr. Buller.

Mitcham noted their reaction. "An unexpected and most unfortunate problem has arisen, and it concerns Mr. Buller. I have called this meeting to report to you the facts of the problem which emerged yesterday, and to seek your advice on appropriate courses of action." Amanda and Stephen exchanged glances. Mitcham, they knew, as they had been invited to the wedding, was shortly to become Mr. Buller's son-in-law. They could not believe that there was trouble afoot.

Mitcham, conscious that he had the undivided attention of everyone present, took a deep breath. "Yesterday, at about 11.30am., two of Mr. Buller's clients, a Miss Rudd and a Miss Dixon, telephoned the office and asked for Miss Turvey. They knew that Mr. Buller was on holiday, but they wanted to complain that they had not received the money due to them following the sale of their property. They were expecting a sum in the region of £35,000, and said that Mr Buller had promised that a cheque would be posted to them before he went on holiday. It had not arrived. Miss Turvey looked for their file, but could not find it. It was then that Miss Turvey reported the problem to me. The client account of Miss Rudd and Miss Dixon shows that on the 16th April a cheque was drawn debiting their account with the sum of £35,000 in favour of the Assurance Bank. Enquiries have revealed that Mr Buller arranged for Rose to deliver the cheque to the Assurance Bank by hand. Apparently, the cheque was in an envelope, which also contained a hand-written note signed by Mr. Buller. Mr. Buller directed Rose to deliver the envelope to Mrs. Green at the Bank, which she did. The note instructed the Bank to pay the cheque into Mr. Buller's private Bank account with Assurance Bank."

Mitcham noted a sharp intake of breath by his partners. "It seems to me that there has been a breach of Solicitors' Account Rules, and that the firm's client Bank account is short by the sum of £35,000. It follows that the firm must pay the sum of £35,000 into the client Bank account immediately in order to eliminate the deficit."

Mitcham paused for a moment to allow his partners time to digest the news. Continuing, he said, "Yesterday afternoon I telephoned Mr Buller, who is staying at the Imperial Hotel in Salcombe, and told him what had happened and what I had discovered. I asked him to come back immediately to put the matter right. He refused, saying that he would attend to it when he returned to the office on Monday. I asked him to telephone the Assurance Bank and instruct the Bank to transfer the sum of £35,000 from his Bank account into the firm's client Bank account. This was at 3pm. He said that he would do this, but no such payment had been received by close of business yesterday. In the meantime, I have asked the firm's Bank if they would be prepared to make a temporary bridging loan of £20,000 repayable within seven days. This sum together with the £12,000 which we hold in office account and £5,000 of my own money should be sufficient to pay off the deficit on client account, and leave us with a working balance of £2,000. Our Bank do not know about this problem, and I have refused to tell them about it or give any reason for suddenly requiring this bridging facility. They may, of course, have deduced the reason for the loan as they made some enquiries of the Assurance Bank on my behalf."

Conscious that his partners were alarmed, Mitcham proceeded: "Yesterday afternoon, I telephoned Miss Rudd and Miss Dixon and told them that Mr Buller was on holiday until Monday and that I could not find their file. Without it I could not work out the exact sum to which they were entitled. Miss Rudd said that they expected £35,000. They accepted that I was not in a position to do anything without the file, and said that they would wait until Monday when Mr Buller was back."

Mitcham paused, and studied the expressions of disbelief and incredulity on the faces of his junior partners. "Have I missed anything out, Howard?" he turned to his accounts manager, who shook his head. Mitcham continued: "I presume that you have no objection to my arranging a bridging loan?" he enquired.

"You do not seem to have any option," responded Stephen gloomily. Amanda nodded her assent. Diane Jarvis, the conveyancing partner, sighed. The report that Mitcham had given had stunned them. It was unthinkable that their Senior Partner had broken the most sacred of Solicitors' Accounts Rules, indeed probably committed a criminal offence, and in doing so had put the very existence of their firm at risk, and possibly diminished their own career prospects. Even though they were only salaried partners, not equity partners, and therefore did not own any part of the firm, they knew that under Partnership Law they were still liable for all of the firm's debts. And they did not know the extent of the firm's potential liabilities. What was even more worrying was that it was the firm's Senior Partner who had transgressed: it did not augur well for the firm's financial viability, let alone future profitability. They felt betrayed and angry. But they had no one to vent their anger on. Mitcham had behaved honourably in what must have been a devastating situation for him. He had clearly put ethics above self-interest. They realised that they had little option but to support him and follow his lead.

Stephen was the first to speak. "Surely the Assurance Bank must account to the firm for clients' money improperly transferred to them," he opined. "They must be under a duty of care, or hold the money as trustee for the firm. Would it not be sensible to obtain Counsel's opinion, a barrister who specialises in Banking Law?" "Good thinking," responded Mitcham.

None of them had previously engaged a barrister who specialised in Banking Law, so Mitcham returned to his room to obtain the Bar List, a compendium of Barristers itemising their qualifications, specialities, telephone numbers and addresses. On his return to the Board Room he heard heated voices which fell silent on his appearance. They all gazed at Mitcham as he leafed through the book's index to find the section of Barristers' chambers specialising in Banking Law. He selected Manning Court chambers in the Inner Temple and telephoned them. He asked the Clerk, who answered the call, to be put through to a barrister who specialised in Banking Law, and in particular was conversant with Solicitors' Accounts Rules and who was available to give instant advice. The Clerk put him through to Mr Travis. Mitcham explained the problem to Mr. Travis.

Travis listened carefully to what Mitcham told him, making notes in shorthand as the story developed. When Mitcham stopped, Travis immediately advised: "the Assurance Bank hold the sum of £35,000 in trust for the firm of Buller & Mitcham under a constructive trust. The remedy is to apply without delay for an injunction to freeze Buller's private Bank account with them, and then follow that up with an application for an order of discovery in order to trace the sum of £35,000 in case Buller has spent any of it. It is all traceable and recoverable under trust law. But to do so will require a lot of paperwork, and I am engaged on a trial this afternoon and so I am not available. In any case I think that you must first notify the Assurance Bank that you have a proprietary interest in the sum of £35,000 wrongly paid into Mr. Buller's account and that the Bank holds that sum to your firm's account under a constructive trust. You should tell the Bank that you have been advised to apply for an injunction at once to freeze Mr Buller's private account and that you are currently considering this advice. You should also point out to the Bank that the Bank owes a duty of care to your firm in respect of that sum. I suggest that you telephone the Bank and give them formal notice of your firm's proprietary interest in the money and discuss the matter generally with them. You may learn more from them."

"Should I follow that up with a letter confirming this?" Mitcham asked. "No, that will not be necessary as long as you and the Bank agree and note the time and date and particular words used by you in giving formal notice," Travis advised.

"Have you ever before had to deal with a Senior Partner breaking Solicitors' Accounts Rules in this way?" asked Mitcham. "Should I be reporting Buller immediately to the Law Society? Should I be dissolving my partnership with him?"

"No, not at this stage," was the reply. "You should convene a meeting with him, set out the facts as you know them to be, and ask him for an explanation of his conduct. It may be that there is an innocent explanation. Best not to take irreversible steps now in the heat of the moment which you may later regret, or have cause to regret. Wait until you know all the facts and are able to take a calm and considered decision. Assurance Bank will not disclose to you whether your partner's private account with them is good for £35,000 because of customer confidentiality, but your firm's Bank should be able to elicit this information from them."

Mitcham thanked him for his advice, and replaced the telephone receiver. His colleagues had heard the whole conversation on loud speak. Curious faces looked enquiringly at him.

"I agree with Counsel," opined Mitcham, "I think that

we must give Mr Buller the opportunity to explain matters, before we take irretrievable steps. There must be a chance that he will be able to return the £35,000 quickly. On the other hand, we should be prepared to proceed with an application for an injunction. Stephen, do you think that you could prepare a brief for Mr. Travis to draft all the papers necessary for an injunction?" Stephen nodded his affirmation. "Amanda, could you, please, ask Miss Turvey to extract all Mr. Buller's current probate and trust files and hand them to you. I would like you to do an audit of them to see if he has misappropriated any other client monies. Diane, could you please do the same with his conveyancing files?"

"What about the Assurance Bank?" asked Stephen. "Are you going to telephone the Assurance Bank?" "Yes", replied Mitcham, "but first I think that I should speak with Mr. Buller"

It was 10.30 am. when the telephone in their hotel bedroom rang. Buller and Elspeth had consumed their breakfast in a desultory silence; Buller racked in guilt and worry, Elspeth not wishing to disturb his thoughts. They had returned to their room, and had changed into their beachwear ready for a morning lying on sunbeds next to the swimming pool. The sun was shining in a clear blue sky, and Elspeth hoped that its influence would ameliorate his mood. 'Damn the telephone!' she thought savagely on hearing it ring, 'That will wreck our day.'

"Buller speaking," were the next words that she heard. "Oh, Graham. It is you. What do you want?" Buller sounded cross. After a pause, she heard him say, "No, I was not able to get through to the Bank yesterday, so I have posted a cheque made payable to the firm for £35,000. I sent it first class, so if you have not received it today you will get it tomorrow." A pause followed, then, "No, after yesterday's experience of wasting time and several telephone calls trying to contact Mr. Johnson at the Bank, I am not prepared to waste more time in trying to contact him to ask him to organise a telegraphic transfer. As I am sure you will appreciate I have made amends by sending a cheque to the firm for the full amount, to put right this mistake on my part. I am on holiday, and I am not prepared to spoil my holiday and Elspeth's holiday to attend to an office matter which I can sort out on Monday." Buller was perspiring as, summoning all his power of ebullience, he sought to fob off Mitcham.

A further pause ensued, whilst Elspeth unsuccessfully sought to hear what Mitcham was saying. "You have done what?" Buller screamed down the telephone. "You have convened a partners' meeting without notifying me? And told them all about this unfortunate mistake on my part? Are you stark raving mad? Or," he spluttered in rage, "have you got another agenda?" He spat out the last words with uncharacteristic venom, which shook Elspeth and the partners sat around the Board Room table.

108

Taken aback by the fury of his words, Mitcham meekly replied: "Surely the best thing to do, John, is to return immediately to the office and sort this problem out to the satisfaction of our partners and myself." "You have a nerve, Graham," Buller blustered. "I will see you all on Monday. Good day." With that, he slammed the telephone down on to its cradle, his body quivering with emotion. He stood glowering at the telephone until Elspeth gently took his arm in her hand, and soothingly entreated him to take it easy on himself and come out with her to sunbathe. Sheepishly now, Buller, his anger slowly abating, lowered his shoulders and allowed himself to be ushered out of the room.

Mitcham surveyed his colleagues. "I think that I ought now to ring Mr. Johnson of the Assurance Bank" he said.

Mr. Johnson was surprised to learn that Mr. Mitcham was on the line. They had met briefly on a number of occasions, but did not really know one another. He had a year or so previously tried to pitch for the business of Buller & Mitcham, but Buller was not prepared to consider it. Buller had wanted to keep his private Bank account completely separate from his firm's Bank account. After an initial exchange of pleasantries, Mitcham informed him that Buller had posted a cheque drawn on his private Bank account with Assurance Bank in favour of Buller & Mitcham for £35,000. "Would the cheque clear?" Mitcham asked.

"I am afraid that Banking regulations prevent me from disclosing this," Johnson answered breezily, "but I suggest that you ask your Bank to telephone me if you want an answer to that question."

"Thank you, Mr Johnson," Mitcham replied, "I have my partners with me listening to this conversation on loud speaker. The sum of £35,000 that was paid into Mr. Buller's private account with you are client account monies of this firm and should not have been paid into Mr Buller's private Bank account. I am giving you formal notice that those monies belong to Buller & Mitcham's client account and must be returned to Buller & Mitcham's client account at once. Whilst the sum of £35,000 remains with your Bank, your Bank holds this sum as constructive trustee for Buller & Mitcham."

Mr. Johnson interjected, "Right. I have made a note that on Wednesday 12th May at 11.15 a.m. on behalf of Buller & Mitcham you gave notice to the Menston branch of the Assurance Bank that the sum of £35,000 had been received by the Bank and wrongly paid into the private Bank account of Mr. John Buller, and that the Assurance Bank is deemed to hold the sum of £35,000 as constructive trustee for Buller & Mitcham's client Bank account."

Mitcham was impressed by the efficient tone that Mr Johnson had adopted. Mitcham continued: "We have taken Counsel's opinion on this, and he has advised us to begin injunction proceedings against the Assurance Bank in order to freeze Mr. Buller's account and to seek an order for discovery so that the missing monies can be traced. He has also advised that an action in negligence lies against the Assurance Bank. My partners and I are considering this advice." Johnson's reply was terse: "Noted." With that the conversation concluded.

Mitcham turned to his partners. "I think that that concludes our business for the moment. I will report any developments to you as they happen. Has anyone any questions?" They all demurred. "One final matter," warned Mitcham, "I do not want any of this to be leaked outside this room. The future of this firm and our individual careers depend on this remaining secret for as long as possible. Is that firmly understood? Do I have your undertakings not to talk about this to anyone apart from each other?" They all agreed. "Good," replied Mitcham, "let's get back to work. If anyone has any bright ideas or worries, will they please address them to me in the first instance?" They all nodded, rose from their chairs and filed out of the room. 'It is going to be difficult to keep the lid on this,' Mitcham mused to himself.

At 12.45 pm. Susan and her excited party arrived at the Hotel Ambassador on the Boulevard Haussmann. Located near to the Opera House the hotel exuded style and luxury. Checked in, a porter directed them to their adjacent rooms and delivered their cases. Their rooms were large, well -furnished and inviting. Throwing herself on to a bed, Susan gasped: "Three

111

days of this! What luxury!" A pillow landed on top
of her. Laughing she chased after her assailant.

At 11.45 am. Buller handed an envelope to Reception
addressed to Mr. G. Mitcham, care of Buller &
Mitcham, Solicitors, No. 1 The Market Square,
Menston in which he had enclosed a cheque that he
had written in favour of Buller & Mitcham, drawn on
his private account with the Assurance Bank for
£35,000. There was no covering letter. 'At least this
ought to buy me some time,' he thought without
much confidence. Anger had been replaced by guilt
and self-doubt.

At 11.45 am. Mitcham was seated in a Manager's
room at his firm's Bank, reading through documents
that had been presented for his signature. With a
heavy heart, he picked up his pen, and slowly,
deliberately signed them. Howard witnessed his
signatures. "How do you want the payment to be
made, Graham?" Westlake asked. "By Bank transfer
into the office account of Buller & Mitcham, please,"
was the reply. Mitcham had already transferred the
sum of £5,000 out of his private Bank account into
the firm's office account. "The sum of £20,000 will
be in your firm's office Bank account by the close of
business today," Mr Westlake assured him.

When they had left the Bank, Howard asked Mitcham

why he had not asked Westlake to contact Johnson to find out whether a cheque drawn by Mr. Buller for £35,000 would clear. "I did not want to give him the impression that the firm was in financial trouble, in case he withdrew the offer of the bridging loan," Mitcham replied. "Hopefully tomorrow we will be able to transfer £35,000 out of office Bank account into client Bank account".

After arranging an impromptu partners' meeting to be held at 2 pm., Mitcham took an early lunch. Normally for lunch he consumed a round of sandwiches and an apple in his office whilst he continued working. Today he took his sandwiches and apple to his house. He wanted to make a telephone call, and he did not want anyone at his office eavesdropping. "Dad, I need your help," was his opening remark. Mitcham needed to talk the whole story through to someone who had his best interests at heart; he needed to forewarn him of the potential impact of his office problems with Buller on his coming nuptials with Buller's daughter, and he needed his financial help.

"Dad, I am very worried that we shall not recover anything like £35,000 from Buller. The temporary bridging loan of £20,000 that I have arranged with the Bank expires in seven days' time. I am seeking to arrange a personal loan to cover that sum, but if I am not able to arrange it within that time, I wonder if you and Mum would be able to lend it to me. I will, of course, pay it back with interest, but I do not see who else I can turn to."

This potential problem was a real worry for Mitcham, and his father sensed the desperation in his son's voice. "Leave it with me, Graham," his father answered. "I will make arrangements with my Bank to cover you for £20,000 should the need arise. Your Mother and I will go to see the Bank this afternoon to make the necessary arrangements." Mitcham sighed with relief. "Thank you so much, Dad. You will not tell the Bank anything about what I have just told you," Mitcham added anxiously. "No. You can rest assured on that," his father assured him. "I will let you know how I get on."

At 2p.m. Howard and the partners gathered together in the Board Room. "I thought that you would like to know that I have signed papers with our Bank for a temporary bridging loan of £20,000 and that the loan ought to be in our office bank account by the close of business today," Mitcham assured them. "I have transferred £5,000 of my own money into our office Bank account. So, first thing tomorrow I intend to transfer £35,000 from office bank account into client Bank account. The breach of Solicitors' Accounts Rules will then be remedied. If we receive a cheque from Mr. Buller, I will ask Howard to arrange for it to be specially cleared. If it does clear, then it will be paid into office Bank account to clear the bridging loan and to restore our office account. Any

questions?" he looked around the room enquiringly.
"What about reporting the breach to the Law
Society?" asked Stephen. "I think that we can follow
Counsel's advice and wait until we have heard Mr.
Buller's explanation on Monday," replied Mitcham.
"It is possible that he has a simple explanation,
although I confess that I think it is unlikely. But I
think that we ought to give him the benefit of the
doubt and give him a chance to put matters right."
The others concurred.

Mitcham returned to his room, conscious that he had
to deal with other clients' pressing problems, which
had been necessarily put on hold for the previous
twenty-four hours. Just to sit down quietly and
concentrate on those would be a welcome relief. A
cup of hot tea, thoughtfully provided by his secretary,
was on his desk.

Buller and Elspeth were dozing on sunbeds after a
heavy lunch and copious glasses of red wine. Elspeth
had decided that such a feast would be the only way
that she would be able to free John of his obsessive
worry and make him relax. His heavy snoring proved
that her strategy had been right, although it was
clearly an irritant to other guests scattered around the
swimming pool.

Susan and her friends sauntered down Boulevard Haussmann chattering and laughing as they made their way to the Café de la Paix, situated in the Place de L'Opera opposite the Opera House. There they each ordered a café au lait and sat back to relish the scene. The appraising looks of a group of young men at a nearby table only added to their pleasure. 'This is going to be a wonderful hen party,' Susan reflected, 'one that we shall all remember.' But she was missing Graham. It had seemed a long time since she had spoken to him even though it was less than twenty-four hours ago.

Although they had promised not to speak with one another during the hen party, she wondered whether she could maintain this. Perhaps tonight, if she can steal away from her friends for a few minutes, she could telephone him and tell him all her news and hear his loving voice again.

At 5 o'clock Howard knocked on Mitcham's door, and poked his head round the opening door. "£20,000 has been credited to office account," he announced with a smile. "Thank the Lord," declared Mitcham. "I will prepare a requisition slip for tomorrow. At least that problem is resolved," he exclaimed with relief. "Tonight, I shall celebrate with a steak and a pint of beer," he promised himself. His thoughts turned momentarily, but sadly to Susan.

He worked until 8.30 pm. trying to catch up on his clients' work. He then slipped out of the office, after setting the office alarm and locking the heavy front door behind him. A few minutes later he was sat at a table at his usual pub, a pint of beer in his hand and a fillet steak on order, his mind mulling over the astonishing events of the past two days. As he relaxed, he wondered whether he had been too precipitate in his actions. Had he been fair to John, had he jumped too readily to conclusions, worse still had he drawn the wrong conclusions? Should he not have readily agreed to leave the matter of the deficit on the Rudd and Dixon account until Monday to allow John to sort it out? After all that was all that had been achieved, and the clients had understood the position and agreed to wait until Monday for John to sort it out. Had he panicked? Was it all just a dreadful mistake, from which he had drawn unfair inferences? Had he thereby sullied the firm's reputation with two Banks: the firm's bank and the Assurance Bank?

He stirred uneasily, and ordered another pint. And what would be the impact of this horrible saga on his future relations with John? He had never before doubted the honesty and integrity of John, and could not believe that he was capable of misappropriating his clients' money for himself. It really was unthinkable. Yet that was what he had suggested, or at least implied, to John, and to his partners, was what John had done. And John had proved himself to be so supportive of Mitcham in the past. 'He would make an ideal father-in-law,' Mitcham reflected. 'Oh dear,

117

what have I done? What damage have I caused?
What effect will this have on my engagement to
Susan?' Mitcham agitated as he considered the
intricacies of his plight. When would she learn about
his false accusation? No doubt before their wedding
day. Mitcham shuddered. Would she still marry him
after all this? Would John tell her? And yet there had
been the issue of a deficit of £35,000 on the client
Bank account. Solicitors' Account Rules required the
partners to rectify the shortfall as soon as it was
discovered. This he had done. But had he been over
zealous? Troubled and anxious, Mitcham regarded
his fillet steak, which had been placed in front of him,
warily. "Oh dear," he sighed.

Mitcham had just settled into his bed when his
bedside telephone rang. Picking it up, he quickly
realised that he had an excited Susan on the other end.
"Oh, Graham. I know that we said that we would not
disturb one another whilst I was on my hen party, but
I just have to hear your voice. I am missing you so
much, I simply have to hear you, to feel you close to
me!" Mitcham gathered his thoughts quickly.
"Susan, it is so wonderful to hear you! I am missing
you desperately too! How is the party going? What
have you been doing?" he gushed.

Susan excitedly related the events of her day,
describing their accommodation and their tour of
Paris that afternoon on a "hop-on hop-off" bus. In
sotto voce, in case any of her friends overheard her,

she divulged the confidences and the stories that she had learned. Happily and excitedly they talked, until suddenly Susan exclaimed that she could hear footsteps approaching and that she must ring off. Graham heard her burst out laughing as a wet flannel hit her face, and whispering "I love you, darling," she terminated her telephone call.

Graham slumped back on to his bed, relishing her excitement and recalling all that she had said. "I love you," he whispered to Susan's smiling face in her portrait. "Oh! I do hope that nothing prevents us from marrying," he muttered.

Thursday 13th May 1982

Mitcham completed the requisition form transferring the sum of £35,000 out of the office bank account into the client Bank account. He signed it, and took it to the Accounts department where Howard gladly received it. He then descended the stairs, and entered the Board Room where the day's delivery of post was piled on the table waiting to be opened. On top was an envelope addressed to a Mr. G. Mitcham, bearing the logo of the Imperial Hotel at Salcombe. Mitcham tore it open. Inside was an Assurance Bank cheque drawn on the account of J. Buller for £35,000 made payable to Buller & Mitcham and signed by J. Buller. There was no covering letter. 'Thank God,' thought Mitcham, 'let's hope that it will clear.' He pressed the intercom. "Howard, can you please come down to the Board Room. I have a cheque for you." He continued opening and sorting the post between the various departments. When Howard entered the room, he asked him to close the door, and then handed him the cheque. "There was no covering letter with the cheque," he remarked. "Can you please take the cheque to our Bank and ask them to do a special clearance on the cheque."

An hour later, Howard knocked on Mitcham's office door and entered. "I have taken the cheque to our Bank and asked them to do a special clearance. The clerk said that they would "run it" specially round to the Assurance Bank and telephone me with the result." "We will keep our fingers crossed," said Mitcham. Howard nodded grimly.

Half an hour later Howard was back in Mitcham's room. "The Home Bank have just telephoned me asking when we are going to discharge the mortgage that Miss Rudd and Miss Dixon have with them on the property which they have sold. Apparently, Miss Rudd and Miss Dixon had called into the Bank to check that their mortgage had been redeemed. It had not been paid off, and was accruing daily interest. The figure required to pay off the mortgage as at today's date is £6,312."

Mitcham groaned. "I will requisition a cheque to discharge it, Howard," reaching for his requisition pad. A few minutes later he was in the Accounts room, signing a cheque in favour of the Home Bank for £6,312, which he handed to Howard. "Can you please take it straight to them, Howard. I will telephone Miss Rudd and Miss Dixon, and thank them for drawing the Home Bank's attention to this, and that I have just sent you with a cheque to the Home Bank to discharge the mortgage." Mitcham then telephoned Miss Rudd to report that he had just discharged their mortgage, adding that the extra interest unnecessarily incurred would be paid by Buller & Mitcham, and not by them.

At noon, there was a knock on the door. A grim-faced Howard entered the room and closed the door behind him. "The cheque bounced," he announced with no further elaboration. "Damn!" exclaimed Mitcham. "Damn, damn, damn!"

Mitcham telephoned the Imperial Hotel and asked the receptionist to put him through to Mr Buller. "Oh! You have just missed them. I saw them leave the hotel about half an hour ago. They said that they were going to the races at Exeter for the afternoon. They said that they will be back in time for dinner." Mitcham swore under his breath. "Thank God we arranged the bridging loan," he observed to Howard. "This is serious."

Half an hour later Howard was back in Mitcham's room, his face flushed. "Sit down, Graham," he commanded Mitcham, who was standing, deep in thought, looking out of his office window. Mitcham turned enquiringly. "Sit down," Howard repeated.

121

Mitcham did as he was ordered.

"There is another one," Howard reported to the startled Mitcham. "Since I saw you a little while ago the Criterion Bank have telephoned me to ask when they may expect payment of £45,000 in the estate of D.E. Stewart deceased. Miss Turvey cannot find that file either. The client account of D.E. Stewart deceased shows that a cheque for £45,000 was paid on the 18th March this year to the Assurance Bank. There is no other money in the account."

Mitcham grimaced in pain. Nervous tension swept through him, his stomach hurt. "Oh, no!" he winced, "Oh no!" "And Amanda has just informed me that she has discovered a withdrawal of £10,500 on the client account of G. West deceased. Again, the client account shows that this was paid to the Assurance Bank, and the file cannot be found. I am afraid that we are facing a big problem."

Mitcham dispensed with lunch. He convened an emergency meeting of the partners for 2 pm., at which he reported the up to date position to a dispirited panel of partners. "I have decided that I shall go this afternoon to Salcombe to interview Mr. Buller. Howard, I would like you to come with me if you will be so good. I am sorry if it will cause you any inconvenience, but your presence will be invaluable. I really do not think that I can handle this on my own, and besides there ought to be a witness present." Howard readily agreed to go. It was agreed that they would leave Menston at 5pm., for Mitcham had an afternoon of appointments with clients ahead of him which could not be cancelled. 'I can see spending the whole weekend at the office working to catch up,' Mitcham brooded ruefully.

Mitcham telephoned the Imperial Hotel at Salcombe to reserve two single rooms for the night. He was in luck; the hotel had two such rooms available. Mitcham ordered a cold buffet to be prepared and left in their rooms. They would be arriving at about 10 o'clock, he told them. After seeing his last client, Mitcham signed his post, told his secretary that he would not be in the office until Monday and to cancel any appointments that he had with clients for the following day. He filled his briefcase with Lindley on Partnership Law, paper, pens, envelopes and stamps. He then left the office, and drove back to his house. There he hurriedly packed an overnight bag. He then returned to the office where Howard was waiting for him. Much to Mitcham's relief, Howard elected to drive the firm's car. Mitcham sat back in the passenger seat, and closed his eyes. It was going to be a long night and he wanted to think, if possible to sleep.

Buller and Elspeth returned to the Imperial Hotel earlier than they had planned. They had enjoyed a picnic at the Exeter race course, tucking into the hamper with which the hotel had supplied them and

123

enjoying the bottle of Sauvignon Blanc which had accompanied it. The sun had shone, and Elspeth had won bets on two races. Buller had been able to cast off his worries and relax. In such a frame of mind they had returned to the hotel, and after taking a bath, had dressed for dinner. An early night beckoned. Elspeth was relieved to observe that John was more like his usual self, less self-preoccupied than he had been for the past two days.

Susan and her friends spent Thursday morning in the Louvre, wandering through gallery after gallery, admiring beautiful paintings. They elbowed their way through the throng of people in front of the Mona Lisa to study her elusive smile and the artistry of the painting. A bus ride to the Eiffel Tower followed, and they savoured the view of Paris from the viewing gallery of the Tower. A quick snack at a café was a necessary precursor to an assault on the Galeries Lafayette, a mega shopping store on the Boulevard Haussmann.

Worn out by the excitement and the exertions of the day, Susan and her friends returned to their hotel. There they all collapsed on to their beds for a nap, conscious that they were going to eat a large dinner in the hotel restaurant that evening. They wanted to look their best and they did not want to be tired.

CHAPTER TEN

Flat Midlands countryside gave way to Cotswold hills, and distant views of the Malvern Hills, as the car sped along the M5 motorway towards the Bristol Channel. Howard enjoyed driving cars, and it was no hardship for him to drive Mitcham down to Salcombe. He looked across at the dormant figure of Mitcham. They had scarcely spoken all journey. Only two hours driving lay ahead, and then he would be able to devour a delicious cold buffet before going to bed. He promised himself a beer. On past Exeter towards Totnes, where they stopped for a coffee at a quaint coffee house. Refreshed they drove through narrow country lanes towards the Salcombe Estuary.

By the time they reached the Imperial Hotel sunlight had disappeared and the estuary was barely discernible in the gloom. Howard parked the car in the hotel car park, opened the car boot and extracted their suitcases. They walked into the hotel, both hoping that they would not bump into Buller and Elspeth. Formalities completed, they collected the keys to their adjoining rooms, and took the lift to the first floor where their rooms were to be found. They were pleasantly surprised by the furnishings of their rooms and particularly by the large buffet which Mitcham had ordered. They ate together in Mitcham's room, the buffet washed down by a glass of beer. The time was 10.30 pm.

"Time to turn in," said a relaxed Howard. "Eh!" exclaimed Mitcham, "No. I want to interview Buller now." "What now?" Howard was astounded. "Yes. Now." Mitcham was cold and determined. Adrenalin was running through him: he was not going to waste any time in getting to the truth, to find out what Buller was up to, and the scale of the disaster that lay before him. Besides he wanted to catch his quarry off his guard. He telephoned the receptionist and ascertained the number of the room in which Buller was staying and its telephone number.

Buller had just fallen asleep when the telephone on his bedside cabinet rang. He stirred unwillingly into consciousness, as Elspeth shifted uneasily beside him. He lifted the receiver in a daze, and said, "Buller speaking".

"John, I am at the hotel and I want to see you in the hotel lounge in five minutes' time." "Who is this?" replied Buller, vaguely thinking that the caller sounded like Graham Mitcham. But Mitcham was safely miles away in Menston. "Mitcham" was the curt reply. "But, Graham, do you know what time it is? I am in bed. And, anyway, where are you?" "In your hotel, Room 12, and I want to see you straight-away." "What? You are here in the Imperial Hotel at Salcombe?" Buller spluttered in disbelief. Then, pulling himself together, he said firmly, "No, Graham, I am not going to be disturbed tonight. I will see you in the morning."

Mitcham did not hesitate. "If you are not in the hotel

lounge in ten minutes' time, John, I shall call the Police. Now which is it to be?" Mitcham heard Buller swear quietly to himself. "I will see you in the lounge at 11 o'clock," replied Buller, trying to seize some initiative in what was fast becoming a desperate situation.

Mitcham could hear Elspeth's exasperated voice in the background, "John what on earth is going on? This is getting out of all proportion!"

The lounge was vast, semi-circular in shape. It was deserted. Graham selected a corner where he could see anyone approaching or eavesdropping. He arranged three chairs around a large coffee table. Howard placed his large ledger of client accounts on the table. They sat down, waiting for the arrival of their quarry.

Faraway at her hotel, an inebriated Susan dialled Mitcham's home telephone number. It was not answered. She was surprised. Although they had not arranged to speak that evening Susan had assumed that they would do so before they retired to bed. She tried again, but with the same result. So, she left a message on his answerphone, saying that she had tried to telephone him, that she had enjoyed a wonderful day, and a lavish dinner at the hotel, that she hoped that he was all right and that she loved him very dearly. "Sweet dreams, my darling," she whispered to her photograph of him propped against her telephone on her bedside cabinet.

At 11 o'clock Buller sidled nervously into the lounge. He looked around the deserted lounge to check that no one else was there. 'This is all very embarrassing and unnecessary,' he thought. He was surprised to see that Mitcham was accompanied by Howard. "What on earth do you mean, coming down here, disturbing my holiday, dragging me out of bed at this time of night?" he demanded of Mitcham. "And what do you mean by bringing Howard here? This is all quite absurd." He had decided that attack was the best course for him to take. "And Elspeth is none too pleased about being woken up at this time of night, either." 'That no doubt is true,' reflected Mitcham as he beckoned at Buller to sit down.

Mitcham allowed Buller a minute or so to compose himself. Then he launched his exocet. "John, you have lied to me. I want to hear no more lies from you, no more deceit. The cheque for £35,000 which you sent to me bounced. It is clear that you deliberately misappropriated that sum from the account of Miss Rudd and Miss Dixon. We have learned today that you have withdrawn £45,000 from D.E. Stewart deceased and paid it into your private account. We also know that you have misappropriated £10,500 from the estate of G. West deceased. So, no more lies, please. I want the truth.

I want to know who else you have defrauded, so that I can start to repair the damage that you have caused."

Buller was stunned. He nervously looked around the lounge. Still no one else there. He looked at Mitcham. Mitcham was glaring at him. "But, Graham..." he started. Mitcham interrupted him: "Now, let us start at the beginning. You took £35,000 out of the client Bank account and paid it into your private account with the Assurance Bank. Why did you do this? Why was there not sufficient money in your account to pay this sum back to the firm? Where has it gone?" He glared at Buller. Buller refused to answer. "You said that you would sort out payment to Miss Rudd and Miss Dixon on Monday. How are you going to do this? Whose account are you going to pillage in order to pay them out?" Buller looked straight ahead, saying nothing. "Well, then, why did you withdraw all the money from the client account of D.E. Stewart deceased and pay it into your private account, some £45,000?" There was no answer. "How were you going to repay it? Were you going to pay it out of the monies you had misappropriated from Miss Rudd and Miss Dixon?"

"Graham. What on earth is going on?" Out of the shadows emerged an incandescent Elspeth. "This is outrageous. Why are you here? Do you know what time it is?" Mitcham looked at her, and thought hard. 'Perhaps if I tell her the facts, it will prompt John into telling me the truth,' he decided. Turning towards her he said, "Elspeth, it hurts me to have to tell you this but as you demand to know what is going on, I will

129

tell you. I am here because John has misappropriated the sum of £35,000 from clients of our firm, and paid it into his private Bank account. This is not only a breach of Solicitors' Accounts Rules, but a criminal offence. I know of two other similar cases where he has misappropriated clients' money, and I need to know what other cases there are, so that I can start to put matters right. Now you will understand the nature of this meeting and its urgency. I shall be pleased if you will now go back to bed. John will join you once he has told me everything. If he does not, then I will call the Police."

Elspeth stared hard at Buller, then turned on her heels and swept out of the lounge. Outside the lounge, she began to swoon as the full impact of what Mitcham had told her began to sink in. Her legs buckled under her, and she slumped against the wall. A wail emitted from her lips. Howard sprang to his feet and rushed out of the lounge. He found Elspeth slumped on the floor, crying noiselessly. He pulled a handkerchief out of his pocket and handed it to her. She took it gratefully, dabbed her eyes, and allowed Howard to pull her to her feet. "I will escort you to your room, Elspeth," he offered, but she assured him that she would manage on her own. He watched her stumble off into the lobby and then to the lift. Once in her room she threw herself on to her bed and wept uncontrollably.

As Mitcham had anticipated, Buller wilted under this unexpected pressure. It was too much to take. To be humiliated in front of Elspeth was more than he could

130

bear. "Graham was that necessary?" he demanded. "You gave me no choice," snarled Mitcham. "Now I want answers to my questions. Otherwise I will call the Police," he added brutally.

Buller melted. He knew that Mitcham would not give up. He also knew that time had run out for him, that his initial unintended misappropriation of monies from various clients' accounts over the years had spiralled out of control, that he had probably reached the end of the road. It had all become unmanageable; as the events of this week, his first week's holiday away from the office for many months, had shown. He had had to placate impatient, sometimes angry clients by paying them excessive amounts of interest. He did not know how much his accumulated debt on clients' account was, but he knew that it was beginning to be difficult to identify large enough sums from unsuspecting clients to cover other clients' demands. In the early days, it had been easy to raise a cheque on a client's account made payable to the Assurance Bank and to have it credited to his private Bank account. But not anymore. It had been a simple ruse at the outset. The client Bank account balance always balanced with the firm's total client account balance, so the accountants were not able to pick it up on audit. His only risk was if they asked to see a file, but even a file could be doctored if necessary. And the monies appropriated in this way had helped him to finance his family's expenditure in the times when the firm was struggling to survive; before Mitcham had joined the firm and started to inject life into the firm and to turn it around.

Mitcham's arrival had been a godsend, a chance to put right his misappropriations, but it had been too late. The accumulated debt was too big to cover out of salary and drawings. He looked wearily at Mitcham. 'God, what a mess I have made of my life,' he thought.

Mitcham sensed the time for the kill was now. "John, I want the whole story now." Buller continued to consider his options, but could see no way for escape from his predicament. He nervously looked around the room, and then from Mitcham to Howard, and then from Howard to Mitcham. "I have here, in the ledgers, all the client accounts with which you have been involved, past and present, John," said Howard firmly but in a confidential tone of voice. "I suggest that you and I do a trail through these to see what has happened." Buller nodded resignedly, and Howard turned his chair so that he was next to him. Howard opened the ledger, and leafed through it until the client account of Rudd and Dixon appeared.

Mitcham sat back, content for the moment to leave it to Howard to do the questioning. He took his notebook out of his case and started to record the conversation in shorthand. Buller was slow in admitting misappropriations, prevaricating and pretending that he could not remember. But Howard was persistent and sharp in his questioning, relishing the opportunity to show his skill and to assuage any doubts that he felt Mitcham may have of him for not exposing the frauds at the outset. For Howard, by now, knew that he had been duped by Buller for many years, and he worried that Mitcham might think that he had been ineffectual in managing the firm's accounts. There were lessons that he needed to learn, and to do so he needed to know how Buller had been able to perpetrate the frauds so successfully over such a long time. So, by challenging Buller's answers, showing at times that his answers did not correlate with the postings in the accounts, he wore Buller's resistance down.

By 1 a.m. Buller had admitted misappropriating monies from the Rudd and Dixon account, the D.E. Stewart deceased account, the G. West deceased account and three other accounts. The shortfall totalled £108,500. They had gone back two years. Buller, implausibly, asserted that he had disclosed everything. Both Mitcham and Howard knew that this was untrue. But it was clear that Buller was struggling. He was too tired to endure any more questions. 'We have enough evidence of wrong doing,' Mitcham thought. 'It may be counterproductive to continue.'

He was about to close the interview with a view to resuming it in the morning, when Buller astonished him. "Elspeth and I are due to meet an old friend and his wife for dinner tomorrow evening. He is a very wealthy landowner. I am sure that he will lend me £50,000 if I ask him tomorrow. That and the money in my capital account will cover the deficit. I will sever the partnership and take my own clients away with me and start a new firm of my own. You will be free of me and these problems, which will no longer exist."

Mitcham was taken aback by the audacity of the proposal. "But how do you know that your friend will lend you £50,000 just like that?" he countered. "Oh, he will" was the reply. "He is a very dear friend of mine. I have no doubt at all that he will lend it to me. I will offer him a first charge on my house. It is free of mortgage, so there is plenty of security for a loan of £50,000." Mitcham was incredulous. "But the misappropriations have already happened, John, on Buller & Mitcham's watch. They cannot be undone."

Silence fell. It was 1.30 a.m. Too late to continue, Mitcham thought. "When do you propose asking your friend for the loan?" asked Mitcham sarcastically. "Oh, between 10 and 11 o'clock in the morning, after breakfast." Buller brightened, sensing the possibility of an escape.

Mitcham looked at him askance. "I will give you an ultimatum, John. By noon you will either have disclosed full details of all your frauds going back to the very first one, or have borrowed £50,000 from your friend. If you do neither of these, I will call the Police. Is that understood?"

Mitcham put his notebook into his briefcase, rose to his feet and marched out of the room. Howard followed. Buller watched them leave the lounge with baleful eyes. 'What on earth am I going to tell Elspeth?' he wondered. He slowly stood up, and

134

staggered out of the lounge.

Mitcham returned to his bedroom. Tired out, he undressed slowly, thinking savagely about the information gleaned from Buller that evening. He caught sight of the framed photograph of Susan which he had earlier placed on his bedside table. Oh, how he missed her! How he needed her! Needed her right now! But had he lost her? Time would tell. "Damn Buller," he cursed.

Any hope that Buller had that Elspeth would be asleep was immediately dashed as he quietly opened their bedroom door. A tear stained Elspeth was sitting up in bed. 'Oh, God!' he thought, 'Now what?'

"John, what is all this about?" Elspeth demanded accusingly. "What have you been up to?" The hapless Buller sat down on a chair, and slowly took off his shoes. 'What the hell do I tell her?' he asked himself.

Buller and Elspeth endured a tortuous night. Elspeth was adamant that Buller confess everything to her, so that she knew the worst and could best advise him. Buller had hesitated to do so, but she persisted until he could withstand her no longer. He wept as he confessed that he had been transferring monies from

135

various clients' accounts into his private bank account for many years (he could not bring himself to use the words "steal" or "defraud" to describe his actions), that he had made a mistake in joining Buller & Mitcham which was in decline and which could scarcely pay him a living salary and certainly not one that could meet his family commitments. He should have left the firm and started afresh, but by then he had appropriated, out of financial necessity, a small sum to cover an unexpected family expense. This had to be paid back before he could think of leaving the firm. But his salary did not provide enough to repay the amount he had taken. Nor was his salary sufficient to produce a loan sufficient to repay the shortfall. Then, again out of financial necessity, he had taken some more money out of a deceased's estate. Now he had two shortfalls to cover.

His bereavement caused him additional expense, for he had decided to send Susan to a private boarding school during the week, as he could not cope with looking after her during the working week. When it became necessary to repay the first debt, he was obliged to do so by transferring moneys from another client account into his private Bank account, in order to release monies from his private Bank account to repay the first debt. The interest that he paid to the first client was so generous that the first client did not quibble over-much about the delay in repayment. Buller had assured the client that in order to earn such a high rate of interest he had had to agree to a six months' notice period, hence the delay in making repayment. But for Buller this Ponzi approach to interest increased his overall indebtedness, putting his ability to regularise his position further away. And so, his illegal trading in clients' money continued, until the present day. Tearfully he confessed that it had spiralled out of control, and that he was finding it unmanageable. The sums now were too big to cover easily, and often he was having to dip into several accounts at once to cover one deficit. It had become a nightmare.

Elspeth listened carefully to his admission. She had a mix of emotions. One was anger at what he had done. And anger at his consequential deceit towards her, masquerading as an honest, upright solicitor with substantial means whereas in fact he was stealing from clients in order to maintain his seemingly affluent lifestyle. A frightening concern was that she now knew of his crimes, his guilt, and if she did not report him to the Police she was no better than an accessory to a crime. This last thought made her shiver. And yet, despite all that she had learned about him in the past hour, she could not deny that she still felt love for him.

As she pondered about her new predicament, Buller took her aback, by declaring his undying love for her, and suggesting that they get married. His proposal caught her off guard. Normally she would have been thrilled to become engaged to the man she loved, but now she was very uncertain. Could she cope with the trials which would undoubtedly follow in the wake of his guilt, the ostracism following his humiliation?

He then surprised her by suggesting that he might be able to borrow £50,000 from their wealthy friend. "No, you must not do that," she ruled, "that would be too embarrassing. What if he refused to lend you the money? It would mean that our friendship would never be the same again. In fact, just asking him would have that effect. It diminishes us. And anyway, where would you get that amount of money to pay him back?" Buller realised with a sigh that that course, however appealing to him, was not available.

They continued to discuss options. Buller realised that he could not continue in partnership with Mitcham. The damage done to their professional relationship was irreparable. But he still thought that a viable career was open to him provided that he could pay off the deficit and Mitcham did not report him to the Law Society. He could announce an amicable dissolution of their partnership, take his clients with him and start again. He could work for another ten years and then sell his business. The proceeds could provide for his retirement. Now if Elspeth would marry him, sell her house and they pooled their income and capital, they could function very well together. Elspeth after all had been pressing him for some time to commit himself to marrying her. It had been he who had been stalling. If he could come to some financial arrangement with Mitcham, he was certain that the whole mess could be swept under the carpet. It dawned on him that the answer would be to give Mitcham his house and all his assets, apart from his pension provision. His house was mortgage free, his wife's endowment policy had secured that. His house must be worth some £70,000 and then there was his car, his furniture and some £50,000 in his capital account with the firm. Surely Mitcham would accept that, and agree not to take matters further. After all, such a solution would save the wedding between Susan and Mitcham, an issue about which he felt deeply guilty. Although he knew that Mitcham would never respect or trust him again, he would not want to lose Susan if it were at all possible. There was a light on the horizon after all. So, he discussed this course, the pros and the cons, with Elspeth.

Elspeth was deeply shocked by what she had learned about Buller. She had admired and respected him all these years as an upstanding pillar of the local legal community, only to discover that it was all based on fraud. It was humiliating. It was disastrous. That this man, with whom she had fallen in love and had enjoyed so many happy times, was a fraudster shook her to the core. And yet he now wanted to marry her. He had rebuffed her entreaties to marry for all these years, and now that his crimes were exposed and he faced professional and financial ruin, he wanted to marry her.

'What sort of cheapskate does he think I am?' she questioned herself. 'And yet do I abandon a man when he is down?' she asked herself. 'What sort of woman does that make me?' Confused, angry and bitter she listened suspiciously to Buller as he put his proposals to her. 'Are the proposals morally right, are they legal?' she asked herself. And then she realised that not only was her immediate future wrapped up in this detestable man, but so was his daughter's wedding and happiness with Mitcham. If Mitcham could accept such a proposal, would it work? Would it save his wedding to Susan? For she realised that Mitcham's integrity, his drive to find the truth and to try to repay the deficit due to clients, was putting his engagement to Susan in jeopardy. 'What a fine man!' she thought. 'To think that their union could be put at risk by John's deceit and fraud!'

And yet she could understand how his weakness, his lack of moral fibre, had driven Buller into this deplorable plight. Buller was beside himself in self-pity as he sought to explain his behaviour, to woo her and to convince her that his proposed solution would resolve the mess satisfactorily for all concerned. Eventually she succumbed to his proposal, more in the hope that to do so would lessen his stress, and allow sleep to assuage misgivings. So, very late on, they settled down miserably to sleep. Another day awaited.

CHAPTER ELEVEN

Friday 14th May 1982

Despite his fatigue, Mitcham could not sleep.
Adrenalin coursed his veins, nervous tension kept him
awake. He could not stop thinking, thinking about
what he had learned; the implications of that
information; Buller's unexpected proposal; how, if
Buller's friend refused to lend Buller £50,000, he,
Mitcham, was going to cover the shortfall on clients'
account; how this tragic state of affairs would affect
his relationship with Susan; and how was she going to
find out; what would her reaction be? One thing was
clear. His partnership with Buller must be dissolved.
And it followed that there must be a full disclosure to
the Law Society. And Buller must not be allowed to
take any of the firm's clients away with him if he was
serious about starting up a new firm on his own. As
he struggled to contemplate how he was going to
meet the shortfall on clients' account, Mitcham
realised that the only practical solution was for Buller
to transfer ownership of all his property and assets to
Mitcham, whatever they were. Tired and troubled,
Mitcham finally fell asleep.

His alarm woke him up at 7 am. He showered,
shaved and dressed. By 7.15 am. he was at the table,
writing out a Deed of Dissolution of Partnership on
deed paper that he had brought with him. At 8am.
Room Service brought him a cooked breakfast, which
he devoured hungrily. At 9 am. Howard was in his
room, and five minutes later his bedside telephone

141

rang. "Graham, can I see you now?" It was Buller.

It was 10 a.m. French time in Paris, and Susan and her friends were at a café in the Boulevard Haussmann enjoying a breakfast of croissants and coffee and watching people and cars rush by. Susan's thoughts strayed to Graham. She fervently hoped that before the day was over she would be able to hear his voice again, to tell him of her experiences and adventures of the past two days, and to tell him how much she loved him. The party was quieter now than two days' previously. The novelty and excitement of all being together for three days, free of business and home cares, to indulge in escapism, and to swap confidences and shared memories, had been replaced by the effects of tiredness and over indulgence. This would not abate, however. Another day and night in Paris beckoned, before their return to England and sobriety. For tonight Susan had promised her party a surprise.

An exhausted looking Buller entered Mitcham's room. He had felt too tired and stressed to eat breakfast, and had foregone it. He had left Elspeth either asleep or feigning sleep, he was not sure which. He had tried to rehearse how he was going to deliver his proposals to Mitcham but had found it difficult to formulate his thoughts, let alone say them.

He nodded to Mitcham and Howard, and lowered himself into a chair. He noted that Mitcham had been busy writing what appeared to be a legal document, and that Howard had his account ledgers open. He quietly groaned in despair. The moment of reckoning had come.

"Graham. Elspeth and I have been discussing the situation," he started hesitantly. "We have decided that I should not ask my friend for a loan. It is too embarrassing, and, of course, he might not agree to give it. What I propose instead is this. I will leave our partnership, and surrender my capital account, which I think has something in the region of £50,000 in it, to you. I will take all my clients with me and start afresh. My house is free of mortgage and worth about £70,000. I will give that to you and all the furniture in it. I will also transfer to you all other assets that I have, apart from my pension policy and my car. I will not ask for any money for the value of my one-half share of the partnership. I think that, in total, this will cover the shortfall on client account and allow you to ride out the storm. I am very sorry that I have let you down and caused such a mess." He would have added that in return he would ask Mitcham not to report him to the Law Society or the Police, but Howard's presence in the room precluded such a suggestion. There would no doubt be an opportunity during the day when he and Mitcham were alone that he could bring the subject up. He was sure that Mitcham would concur. Mitcham would not wish to risk his engagement to Susan by dishonouring her father, he reasoned.

Mitcham sat back in his chair and looked hard at
Buller. He was not surprised by Buller's proposal, for
he had already concluded that it was the only course
open to Buller. "John, whilst I think that proposal
over, can you please make a list of all the main assets
that you are proposing to transfer to me." He ruefully
thought that in the case of furniture the transfer would
be seamless as far as Susan was concerned, but at
least it would save them money. He produced a sheet
of paper and a pen and handed them to Buller. He
then returned to his document and continued drafting
a Deed of Dissolution of their partnership. He then
drafted a Deed transferring the title of Buller's house
to himself. Finally, he drafted a Deed of Assignment
of Personal Assets.

It did not take Buller long to compile a list of his
main assets. He sat watching Mitcham at work for a
while, partly admiring him, partly loathing him, and
then handed him his list. Mitcham scrutinised the list,
and then turned to Buller. "We did not finish the trail
of your frauds last night, John. I want you to go with
Howard into his room next door and continue your
disclosure. I will join you presently to see how you
are getting on."

After Howard and Buller had left the room, Mitcham
went down to reception to ask if they could have the
use of their two rooms for another night. The hotel
was only too happy to accommodate his request.

On returning to his room, Mitcham completed the

Deed of Assignment of Personal Assets listing the various items in Buller's list, including his private Bank accounts. He noticed that Buller had not included in the list a gold watch which he always conspicuously wore. Perhaps as well, Mitcham thought ruefully. It might have been bought with clients' money. He wondered what he should say if Buller asked him not to report him to the Law Society. He expected such a request. He decided that he would await the results of Howard's continued investigation before giving further thought to this.

At 11 am. Mitcham telephoned Amanda. "Can you, Stephen and Diane go into the Board Room, please, as soon as possible for a partners' meeting. When you are together can you please telephone me on this number." He gave her the hotel's telephone number. "I need to talk to you all."

Fifteen minutes later his telephone rang. The junior partners were assembled in the Board Room. A conference call had been arranged. Mitcham reported to them in detail what had happened to date, what misappropriations Buller had admitted. He told them that the debt to date appeared to be in the region of £108,500, but that amount might increase as Howard continued his investigation. He then told them of Buller's proposal to settle, and that as from 10.30 am. his partnership with Buller was dissolved. Mitcham asked them to send a letter to the firm's Bank notifying the Bank that Mr. Buller had left the partnership and to give formal notice to the Bank that they were not to honour any cheque, whether drawn on office account or on clients' account, bearing Buller's signature.

Discussion ensued on publication of notices, both publicly and to Buller's clients, but, in the end, it was agreed to deal with those issues on Monday. Mitcham told Diane that he was about to fax to her a Deed of Transfer that he had drafted transferring the freehold title of Buller's house to himself. He asked her to obtain office copies of the title register, undertake a search of the title registers, and then check his draft deed before he invited Buller to sign it. Diane said that she would do this immediately. Stephen asked Mitcham whether he was going to report the misappropriations to the Law Society. Mitcham replied that he wanted to complete his investigation before he did so. Mitcham instructed them not to breathe a word of Buller's misappropriations to anyone.

At 11.45 am. Howard entered his room. "Buller says that he owns another property, Graham," he announced. "It seems that he owns number 5 Gordon Close in Stonely, a village near here. Three years' ago, he borrowed £30,000 against it from the People's Bank secured by an undertaking given by the firm to repay it out of the proceeds of sale once it is sold. It seems that the People's Bank have become concerned at the delay in repayment and have been asking him when the property will be sold and the Bank repaid. Buller says that the Land Certificate to the property is in the strongroom, but that the property is not on the market. You had better draft another Transfer Deed."

146

Mitcham nodded disdainfully, reaching for the telephone. He then telephoned Diane at the office, and asked her to find the Land Certificate to the property, undertake a search at the Land Registry, and check the draft Transfer Deed which he was about to fax to her.

No sooner had he done this, but there was a knock on the door of his room. Mitcham opened it to find Elspeth standing outside. She looked haggard. Her face was devoid of make-up, and her eyes were swollen and red. She had obviously been crying. Mitcham invited her into his room and steered her to an armchair. "Graham, you must believe me, but I knew nothing about all this," she implored. "I cannot believe that he has done this. John never confided in me about any of his business affairs. I had the most complete shock last night when you told me what he had done. And he has now asked me to marry him! I cannot believe that all this is happening to me!" Tears began to form in her eyes, and Mitcham proffered a tissue to her.

At that moment, Howard poked his head round the bedroom door. "John has now admitted frauds going back six years, and the amount of the deficit has now risen to £150,000 approximately," he announced. Mitcham and Elspeth both groaned. "Well, hopefully, the value of the cottage at Stonely will cover the increase," Mitcham opined. "What cottage?" enquired Elspeth. "He never told me that he owned any other property."

The telephone rang as Howard returned to his room to continue his interrogation of the hapless Buller. "Hi, Diane," answered Mitcham. "Graham. I have searched the strongroom and John's room, but there is no sign of a Land Certificate. So, I obtained a set of office copy entries from the Land Registry and these show that number 5 Gordon Close, Stonely is owned by a Mrs Raven. There is no mention of a John Buller in any of the registers relating to the property." Mitcham groaned out aloud. No wonder the People's Bank were applying pressure on Buller, he thought. The Bank must have done a search and discovered the same result. "Thank you, Diane," he replied, "please don't bother checking the draft Transfer Deed. It clearly will not be needed."

He turned to the distraught Elspeth who was wringing her hands in desperation. "I do not know what to do," she wailed. "I wanted John to cancel the rest of our stay here and take me home, but he would have none of it. He wants to stay here until Sunday. And we are due to see our friends tonight for dinner. I am not sure that I can face them. Do you know, John was keen to ask them this morning for a loan of £50,000. What madness! I had to dissuade him from doing this. There is no hope that he could ever repay them. I think that that is why he asked me to marry him so that he could sell his house, repay the debt and live with me and off my widow's pension. He has never been interested in marriage before," she added bitterly.

Breakfast finished, Susan and her friends took the
metro to the Palace of Versailles. Along the way
Susan told them that they had to be dressed for dinner
and in the hotel's lounge bar by 6 pm. She did not tell
them what surprise lay in store for them that evening.
As she sat back in her seat, she fondly imagined
Graham hard at work in his office. 'I will telephone
him tonight when we get back,' she promised herself.

Elspeth returned to her room, having told Mitcham
what Buller had revealed to her during the night.
Mitcham ordered a plate of tuna sandwiches to be
taken to her room, and plates of sandwiches for
himself, Howard and Buller. Elspeth telephoned him
to thank him. At 2 p.m. Howard entered Mitcham's
room. "John has gone back to his room. I have
completed the audit trail as far as I can. The frauds
go back twenty years and total some £180,000."
Mitcham gasped. "Twenty years, did you say?
£180,000? I do not believe it! I am ruined." Horror
struck, Mitcham slumped back into his armchair, his
eyes closed, tears welling in his eyes. Howard quietly
left the room. There was nothing more that he could
do, nothing that he could say that would offer any
solace, any comfort for his boss.

Mitcham remained slumped in his armchair. He felt
wretched. The adrenalin, which had kept him going
all morning, had drained away, to be replaced by total
weakness and dismay. He could not believe the

149

reality of what had befallen him. Total disaster beckoned him and he was helpless to deal with it. All that he had ever tried to do was to be a conscientious solicitor, solving people's legal problems, and to be regarded as an upright, law abiding citizen. Nothing fancy, just to do his best for everyone. To break the law was anathema to him. It would just never occur to him. And here he was brought down by avarice and unscrupulous deceit by a man who only a few days ago he held in high regard, was pleased to be his partner, and looking forward to being his son-in-law. It was not only tragic, it was unbelievable, utterly uncomprehendingly unbelievable. Ruin faced him. He would not be able to match this debt from any resources available to him. Bankruptcy was inevitable. His career lay in ruins. Bankruptcy would mean that he would immediately be struck off as a solicitor. He would not be able to practise as a solicitor again. It was humiliating, indefensible. And yet he had done nothing wrong. It was undeserved. How could Buller have done this to him? And how had he got away with it all for so long?

Revenge is a powerful emotion, and slowly Mitcham raised himself out of his despair. He telephoned Directory Enquiries to ask for the telephone number of the Law Society. Coldly he dialled the number, waited until he was put through to the Compliance Officer, and reported that Buller had committed grave breaches of the Solicitors' Accounts Rules. He was asked to put it in writing. He told the officer that he was at a hotel in Salcombe where he had interrogated Buller and obtained these admissions and would make a written report to the Law Society on Monday, when he had returned to his office. He gave notice of the dissolution of the partnership to the officer, and then asked if the Solicitor's Compensation Fund covered losses incurred by transgressions of this nature. The officer cautiously replied that it might be available, but it would depend on the facts.

A knock on the door signalled the return of Buller and Elspeth to his room. Hearing the knock, Howard joined them. The four of them sat down in silence. Mitcham was still reeling from his shock. Buller appeared calm and urbane. Elspeth was embarrassed and awkward. Howard was composed. "Can I now sign the Deeds?" pressed Buller, "Are they ready?" Wearily Mitcham collected the documents and handed them to Buller to read. Buller studied them intently. After reading through them carefully he said that they were in order, and he would sign them.

Mitcham said that they would need an independent witness, and telephoned reception to ask if someone in the office could witness their signatures. The Manager agreed to do so, and Mitcham and Buller left the room and descended the staircase to the reception hall. There the nature and purpose of the deeds were briefly described to the Manager, who in turn watched Buller sign the Deed transferring Buller's house to Mitcham, the Deed of Dissolution of the Partnership, and an Assignment of Personal Assets. He then watched Mitcham sign the Deeds. Finally,

151

the Manager wrote his signature, and full name and address below their signatures as a witness. Mitcham dated the Deeds 'and thanked the Manager. Mitcham and Buller slowly climbed the stairs back to Mitcham's room in complete silence.

"All done," Mitcham announced resignedly, as they re-entered the room. "John has signed the Deeds." Buller sat down in his armchair. "Graham, I have just realised that I have not signed a Deed of Transfer of my cottage at Stonely." "What cottage, John?" Mitcham asked. "My cottage at 5 Gordon Close, Stonely." "You do not own a cottage at Stonely, John." Elspeth screeched. "But you know I do," replied Buller. "I have taken you there." Elspeth gaped. "No, you have not," Elspeth replied tartly. "You have shown me a cottage but you did not tell me its address. I do not know where it is." Mitcham interjected. "John. Diane has examined the title to number 5 Gordon Close, Stonely and you do not own it. The registered proprietor is a Mrs. Raven, and your name does not appear in any of the registers relating to the property." "What? Have we sold it then?" asked Buller, looking desperately at Elspeth. "What do you mean by saying have we sold it?" screamed Elspeth back at him. "You know that I have nothing to do with the cottage, that I know nothing about it." They stared at one another in mutual disbelief and disdain. Buller's face was flushed, his hands trembled, and then his body began to shake. His previous composure had deserted him. He was a wreck.

"I think, Graham, that we ought to leave him alone now," Howard intervened. "I do not think that John can take any more." Mitcham nodded. It was clear that Buller had broken down. Elspeth put an arm around Buller, and encouraged him to stand and escorted him out of the room. Howard watched them as they slowly walked arm in arm towards the lift. "He is a broken man, Graham," he observed as he re-entered Mitcham's room. "Why don't we have a cup of tea, eat some sandwiches, pack and return home? There is nothing more to be done here." Mitcham nodded, and telephoned for room service.

Refreshed and suitcases packed, the hotel paid, Mitcham and Howard climbed into Howard's car and set off for home. "Before we leave the area, let us go and look up number 5 Gordon Close at Stonely," suggested Mitcham. Howard nodded in agreement, and Mitcham extracted the AA Road Atlas from the car pocket and started to look for the route to Stonely. On their way towards Stonely, a Daimler motor car veered towards them in the opposite lane, being driven erratically. It swerved into a left-hand turn as the driver, who had obviously recognised their car, turned to look at them. It was Buller. There was no one else in the car. "God, I hope that he is not looking for somewhere to commit suicide," Mitcham groaned. "That could well be in his mind," agreed Howard.

Thirty minutes later they drove into Stonely and started to look for number 5 Gordon Close. Stonely was a small village and it did not take them long to find Gordon Close. Number 5 was set in a nondescript cul-de-sac of houses. Howard pulled up in front of the house. A house rather than a cottage, Mitcham reflected. "Stay here, Howard." Mitcham ordered. "I will go and find out who lives here." He walked up the driveway to the front door, and pressed the doorbell.

After a few moments, the door slowly opened revealing a middle aged, plump woman. "I am looking for a Mr Buller who, I believe, lives here," he asked.

"No. Mr Buller does not live here," the woman warily replied. She looked askance at Mitcham. Then, after a pause, she added, "I remember now. He was the executor." "Oh, he is your landlord then?" Mitcham asked. "Oh no! We own this house. We bought it off him." "When was this?" asked Mitcham innocently. The lady looked down, deep in thought. "Oh, about eight years ago," she eventually replied. "He was the executor of Joan Gordon deceased. It was after her that the cul-de-sac was named."

Mitcham thanked her and left, noticing that the car parked in the drive was displaying a midwife's parking certificate. He related the conversation to Howard as they drove off. Mitcham marvelled at the depth of Buller's deceit and cunning.

For many miles, Howard and Mitcham discussed all that they had learned in the past twenty-four hours, and the implications arising from their discoveries.

Mitcham reported that he had contacted the Law Society to report his discovery of Buller's misappropriations and what they required him to do. Mitcham asked Howard to contact the firm's accountants on Monday to inform them of the dissolution and to arrange cessation accounts. Strategies and details in random order were discussed; until the subject had become exhausted and they lapsed into silence. Howard concentrated on his driving, and Mitcham turned his thoughts to Susan. How was all this going to affect his relationship with Susan? If Buller committed suicide, would that mean the end of their engagement? Would she blame Mitcham for his death? Even if they married, how would they deal with references to Buller – it would be impossible to cut him out of their lives.

Mitcham felt resigned to the prospect of the end of his engagement to Susan. He could not see how it could survive in any form. He drew the same conclusion to whichever scenario he put: the suicide of Buller, the striking off of Buller from the Roll of Solicitors, the trial and imprisonment of Buller, the bankruptcy and consequent striking off the Roll of Solicitors of Mitcham himself. The answer was the same to each question. There could be no future for his engagement to Susan. Anguish racked his body. How was Susan to be informed of her father's disgrace? Should he telephone her? How should he put it? No answer came readily to him, other than to leave it alone for the time being. He knew that Susan was enjoying the time of her life in Paris, and the last thing he wanted to do was to spoil her pleasure. The truth would emerge in all good time.

CHAPTER TWELVE

Susan, bubbling with excitement, joined her smartly dressed friends in the lounge bar of their hotel. She ordered a bottle of the house champagne, and her friends toasted her health and future happiness. They clamoured to be told where they were going to spend the evening, what the entertainment for the evening would be. But Susan refused to tell them, enjoying her secret. All that she would say was that a limousine had been booked for 7.30 pm. prompt in front of the hotel.

At 7.30pm. the porter beckoned Susan to indicate that the limousine had arrived. The porter ushered the six girls into the limousine; and the chauffeur then set off down the boulevard before setting a route in the direction of Place Pigalle. Gasps of excitement emitted from five young ladies as they realised that the limousine had stopped in front of the Moulin Rouge. "What? Are we going in here?" gasped Jeanette. "We sure are," said Susan as the chauffeur opened the doors for them. Inside the theatre they were shown to a table radiating from the stage. In the middle of the table stood three bottles of champagne, sitting in iced champagne buckets. The table was set for dinner. "Ooh la la!" gasped Harriet. "I planned this because I thought that we might run out of conversation by the Friday evening," teased Susan. "You are kidding!" smiled Charlotte. "Anyway, I have always wanted to watch the Can Can," Susan confessed. "Not suitable for your husband to see," chimed in Jeanette.

By the time he had been dropped off at his house Mitcham was exhausted. As they approached Menston he had thanked Howard profusely for all his hard work and counsel, for his forensic skill while interrogating Buller, which had revealed such startling results, and for driving Mitcham to Salcombe and back. Letting himself into his house, Mitcham poured himself a whisky and ran a bath. Although hungry, he was too tired to eat. An early night beckoned, although he was confident that later on Susan would telephone him to tell him her news. He knew that Susan was taking her friends to the Moulin Rouge. He could visualise their excitement. It would not be a place that he would ever wish to go to. It would always now hold too many poignant memories for him.

At 10.30pm. English time his telephone rang. Mitcham roused himself from his slumber. An excited Susan thanked him for paying for the extra night. She recounted all that they had done during the day, relishing the events of the evening. "The Can Can was particularly daring," she teased Mitcham. "I shall take you there on your 40th birthday to celebrate your coming of age," she promised. "You will be old enough to enjoy it." Mitcham heard himself laugh. It seemed a strange sensation. 'When did I last laugh?' he wondered.

Susan turned the topic to the following evening. "I

expect to arrive in Menston early evening. I think that I shall probably be too tired to want to go out. How about staying in our house for the evening, and I can cook you a steak and we can share a bottle of wine?" "It sounds divine to me," replied Mitcham, mustering enthusiasm. "You sound very tired to me, Graham," enquired Susan concernedly. "Have you had a difficult week?" "Very," was the short reply. "Well, we can celebrate being together tomorrow evening and relax," promised Susan soothingly. "I cannot wait to be in your arms again. I love you so much." With those words, they wished each other 'Good night and sweet dreams.'

Mitcham wondered whether her plans for the following evening would materialise, and, if they did, in what form. He certainly did not think it would be as relaxing an evening as she had promised him. He winced in pain. Pain in the stomach had been a constant condition for the past four days.

Saturday 15th May 1982

Mitcham did not sleep well. He was hurting too much to relax into a proper sleep. By 7.30 a.m. he had showered, shaved and eaten a breakfast of muesli washed down with a cup of real coffee. Revitalised, he telephoned his partners and Howard asking them all to attend a partners' meeting in the office at 11 am. They had all already been alerted to expect such a meeting, and had agreed to be there. He then set down to prepare an agenda and a report for the meeting. So much had been uncovered in the previous twenty-four hours that he was anxious not to miss any detail out.

At 9 am. he telephoned his father who listened anxiously to the long story of disaster that his son related to him. He sympathised with him, not knowing what to say. Clearly his son was able to cope with the stress of the events which were embroiling him, but it was all so outside his own experience that he felt unable to say anything of any value. He promised to inform Mitcham's mother of what he had been told, and asked what his son thought would be the impact of the saga on his son's forthcoming wedding. Mitcham confessed that he did not know, that he had not mentioned any of it to Susan as she had been in Paris with her hen party, that he could not imagine that her father or Elspeth would have telephoned her to tell her, and that he was expecting to see Susan that evening and was dreading the encounter. He had not yet worked out what he was going to say to her. "Best to tell her the full facts. They will all come out eventually anyway, and she will respect you more if you are truthful to her," he counselled. Mitcham agreed forlornly.

At 10 am. Mitcham handed a letter of authority signed by Buller and addressed to the Manager of the Assurance Bank to Mr. Johnson. Mr Johnson's eyebrows rose as he read its contents. The letter of authority gave formal notice to the Bank that Mr. Buller had assigned all his accounts, current and

160

deposit, and all securities that the Bank was holding on his behalf, to Graham Mitcham. Attached to the letter of authority was a photocopy of the Assignment of Personal Assets signed by Buller.

"Most unusual," commented Johnson, who asked what had caused Buller to do this. Mitcham did not reply, but instead handed him a letter signed by Mitcham instructing the Bank not to honour any cheques, credit/debit card payments, or instructions given by Mr. Buller. Johnson undertook to implement this instruction immediately. He looked at Mitcham appraisingly. Normally affable and pleasant to deal with, Mitcham appeared cold and focused. Mitcham rose, and with a curt "Goodbye" marched out of his room. "Not even a handshake," noted Johnson, feeling worried.

At 11 am, cups of coffee in front of them, the partners and Howard were seated around the Board Room table, looking expectantly at Mitcham. He handed them copies of the agenda and his written report. For the next five minutes, not a noise was to be heard as they read and digested the facts in his report. When they had finished, Mitcham told them of his meeting with Mr. Johnson of the Assurance Bank that morning and then asked Howard if he had missed anything out. "Only that our invoice for the hotel accommodation and food was paid out of office account," replied Howard dryly. Mitcham asked if anyone had any questions. Stephen said: "I see that you have reported John to the Law Society. I am glad that you have done so."

Mitcham stood up, and moved to the sideboard, opened the doors and extracted two trays of sandwiches. "I hope that you will not mind eating an early lunch as I want us all to go to John's house afterwards and search it for files and anything else that is relevant to the misappropriations." The partners looked at one another uncertainly. "How will we get in?" asked Stephen. "Elspeth told me that John always keeps a front door key underneath a flowerpot in the porch. Otherwise we will have to break a window."

In a patisserie on the Boulevard Haussmann the six girls chose their sandwiches and brioches for the homeward journey. Gathering their purchases and their suitcases they hailed a taxi for Charles de Gaulle airport. The airport was teeming with people when they arrived. They queued for an interminable time at the check-in desk, followed by a long queue through security. Once through security they quickly found the cosmetic section of the duty-free shop, apart from Susan who sauntered into the liquor section. There she bought a bottle of Moet et Chandon champagne and a bottle of Margaux red wine. Pleased with her purchases, which she intended to give to Mitcham that evening, she joined the others at the gate, who all cheekily asked if they were invited too. "Two is company, six is a crowd," she rejoined.

Reclining in her seat, Susan reviewed the events of

the last few days. Her hen party had been a complete success. One never to be forgotten. She was so happy. And then she shivered with excitement as she contemplated her forthcoming marriage. To be married to Graham was a dream about to come true! Oh, how she wished her father could find a wife who could look after him and make him happy too! He deserved to find happiness. She could tolerate Elspeth, but wondered if Elspeth could give her father the love, support and warmth that he needed. With these thoughts swirling in her mind she drifted off to sleep.

Five cars drove up the leafy, tree lined road, and parked. The road was lined by large Victorian detached houses. The four partners and Howard surveyed Buller's house. It was clearly deserted. They all felt nervous. House breaking was not a skill that they had developed. Mitcham led the way. Pushing open the now familiar gate, he walked up the drive towards the front porch. Several flowerpots lined the sill. He upturned the first one to find a key. "Easy," he thought. The front door swung open easily. They hastily entered. Mitcham allocated rooms to each of them to search. After a casual search of each of them, he took Howard up to Buller's bedroom. Tidy but bare, it looked like the bedroom of a middle-aged bachelor. Mitcham's first conclusion was that there was nothing to be found in there. The room was sparse. But Howard brushed past him, and pulled open the door of one of the two wardrobes. Pulling aside a dressing gown he revealed a stack of files, piled high one on top of another.

"Phew, look at this!" he exclaimed. Mitcham joined him and they picked up files which they recognised belonged to the firm and laid them on the bed. Feverishly they searched through them. All the files belonged to the firm. Howard then opened the other wardrobe. There stacked against the rear wall of the wardrobe were three piles of files. They all belonged to the firm. Mitcham scratched his head in disbelief. Howard strode towards a chest beside the bedroom wall. Pulling up the lid, he revealed a chest full of office files. "I cannot believe it!" exclaimed Mitcham, suddenly realising that the reason for the light being on in the bedroom when he dropped off Susan was not the concern of an anxious, protective father but the guilty reaction of a fraudster who had been disturbed in his work.

A file, innocent in appearance, resting on the dressing room table revealed drafts of letters written to angry or impatient clients of the firm, or to Mr. Johnson and his predecessor at the Assurance Bank. Sitting on the bed, Mitcham studied the file. It became apparent that Buller had been running a separate book of accounts with the Assurance Bank, borrowing against clients' client account balances, or giving undertakings on firm notepaper to repay loans given to him by the Bank. It was all so simple, so brazen, Mitcham thought. A perfect example of teaming and lading, robbing Peter to pay Paul.

Meanwhile Howard had been rifling through drawers in bedside cupboards to reveal recent correspondence between Buller and clients, and Buller and the Assurance Bank. "I cannot believe that he could sleep in his bedroom with all this evidence of his wrongdoing around him," exclaimed Mitcham. Howard agreed that it was extraordinary. Howard called the others in, and they stood around the bed, mesmerised by the discovery.

After a while Mitcham asked them if it would be in order for him to remove the files from the house. "No question about it," answered Stephen. "The files and correspondence belong to the firm. The file that you were reading must also belong to you as John transferred ownership of all his assets to you. In any event, it contains evidence of letters written to the Assurance Bank and to clients on behalf of the firm which are evidence of wrongdoing. It would be wrong to leave them here where they could be destroyed by Buller on his return." "Thank you. I accept your advice," concurred Mitcham who had never doubted his right to seize the files, but wanted to be seen to be asking the right questions before doing so. "I think that we ought to continue searching the house," remarked Howard. "Besides client files, we may find other papers and items, such as credit cards and bank statements which may be of use."

As the others filed out of the room, they heard the front door bell ring. They all froze. The bell rang again. They did not move. Mitcham stealthily tiptoed to the bedroom window, cautiously drew back the curtain and peered out. A middle-aged woman turned away from the front door and walked back along the driveway. She glanced back at the house and then walked to the next-door house. "The coast is clear," said Mitcham quietly.

A few minutes later the telephone rang. They all froze. It continued to ring and they remained stationary. Mitcham was beginning to expect police cars to arrive at any moment, clarions wailing. He hated what he was doing. But no police car arrived, the telephone stopped ringing and they resumed their search. The telephone rang again. Again, they all froze in anticipation. It continued to ring, until finally it stopped. They all resumed their search, conscious that time was running out. 'The sooner we are out of here the better,' thought Mitcham. At last they had searched everywhere; the attic, the conservatory, the kitchen and its scullery, everywhere. They piled their discoveries on to the dining room table, credit cards, Bank statements, sundry correspondence all relating to the firm, including a notebook containing account book entries. They stood around the table examining their find, deciding what belonged to the firm and what was extraneous to their investigation and properly was Buller's property. Underneath the kitchen sink Amanda found a roll of black bags, into which they placed the items which they had decided to take back to the office. Three large, battered suitcases were borrowed, and the firm's files and correspondence were placed in them. When all this was done, Mitcham led them out of the house, carefully locking the front door. He pocketed the key. He glanced casually at his watch. It read 5.30 p.m. He, Howard and Stephen each manhandled heavy suitcases to the boots of their respective cars. Amanda and Diane had already loaded their cars with full black bags. Feeling furtive, guilty that their movements were being watched by suspicious neighbours peering through net curtains, they climbed into their cars and one by one drove off. Except for Mitcham. Overcome by emotion, a cocktail of excitement, adrenalin and guilt, mixed with nostalgia for his passion for Susan, he stopped and looked back to survey the house.

"Graham, oh Graham! How wonderful to see you! How absolutely wonderful!" Graham turned around in amazement, to see his fiancée climbing out of her taxi. "Oh, Graham! What are you doing here, darling? How absolutely wonderful!" she exclaimed, as she rushed excitedly across the road and threw herself into his arms. They embraced one another; she in excitement and passion, he in shock and amazement. They drew apart momentarily, and then flung themselves together in another passionate embrace.

An incessant coughing at their side caused Susan to break away. Realising that the taxi driver wanted to be paid for his services, she rummaged in her purse for the appropriate fare. Mitcham stood uneasily by her side, smiling awkwardly at the taxi driver. The taxi driver paid, Susan turned her attention to Mitcham. "Oh, Graham!" she exclaimed. "How lovely of you to be here waiting for me. I do love you so."

With that remark, she grabbed his hand and led him up the driveway. Graham felt sick. He knew that he was about to say words that he never wanted to say, to shock his fiancée with revelations that he knew she would not want to know, to kill a love that she had for him and that he had for her, to destroy a happiness between them that could never be rekindled. And she was so happy. He steeled himself. He watched her unlock the front door, open it and drag him inside. Pulling himself apart from her, he looked lovingly at her, stroked her face and gently kissed her.

"Darling, there is something that I have to tell you," he stammered as they entered the living room. "I do not want to tell you this, but I must." She looked astonished at him. 'What is he saying?' she agitated. Dismay crossed her visage. Frantically she thought, 'Is he having second thoughts about marrying me, or has he met someone else?' before exploding, "Graham, what is it? What are you trying to say?" Mitcham hesitated. "Don't you love me anymore?" she cried hysterically. "No, it is not that, darling," Mitcham tried to console her. "I love you desperately and always will do. It is just that something terrible happened this week, which makes it impossible for us to proceed with our wedding." Susan gasped. "What? What do you mean?" she cried out. "Are you saying that we cannot get married?" Mitcham blanched.

"It is just that this week I discovered, and I hate to say this but I must, that your father has been misappropriating clients' money. In fact, he has been misappropriating clients' money for some twenty years. Because of this, I have had to dissolve our partnership and report him to the Law Society. You must believe me. I really had no alternative."

Susan reeled back in shock, the blood draining from her face. "I do not understand what you are saying. Don't you love me any longer?" she wailed. Mitcham stiffened as he realised the pain that he was causing his fiancée, but he knew that there was no going back. He could not retract the words that he had spoken. Worse, he had more that he had to say. "Your father has taken some £180,000 from clients and Banks which somehow has to be repaid." Susan gasped. Mitcham continued, "I cannot see how I am going to be able to repay it and I am facing the possibility of bankruptcy. The Law Society is bound to strike your father off the Roll of Solicitors and no doubt will report his misconduct to the police."

Mitcham was trying to choose his words carefully. He did not want to sound too dramatic, so he eschewed words like "stealing, theft and fraud" which would cause unnecessary offence. He concluded sadly, "I cannot see how we can possibly proceed with our wedding until all this horrible mess is over. It just seems impossible to me."

The shock of his revelations was too much for Susan as the meaning of his allegations sunk in. Her body quivered in outrage. "What? What are you saying, Graham? Are you saying that my father is a thief!" She raged at him, her words pouring out in a torrent. "How dare you say such a thing? It is not true. It cannot be true! Why are you saying such wicked lies about him? Why? I cannot believe it of you. How dare you?" With that she threw herself hysterically on to a sofa. "But it is true, Susan," Mitcham protested. He moved towards her to comfort her, but she, like a wounded animal, rejected his advance, screaming hysterically at him. "Go away. Go away. I never want to see you again!"

Mitcham bit his lip, and withdrew quietly, letting himself out of the house. He could hear Susan sobbing. Dejectedly he walked slowly down the driveway to his car, climbed in, looked sadly at the house, and then drove off. He had expected this result, so he was not surprised, but still he felt mortified that by being upright and truthful he had lost the love of his life. Perhaps, he consoled himself, Buller or Elspeth will come to his rescue and vindicate him to Susan. 'Some hope!' he thought.

CHAPTER THIRTEEN

Mitcham returned to his house where he poured himself a whisky, and sat down to take stock of a disastrous, utterly miserable situation. "Take it easy," he told himself, but he was still shocked by her reaction, even though he had anticipated it or something similar. The force of her fury had disturbed him, caught him by surprise. Surely Susan would relent, or would she? Time only would tell. He thought about telephoning her, to say how sorry he was to be the bearer of such harsh news, but thought that such an approach may be premature. Let Susan take soundings and sleep on it, he decided sadly. It certainly was not going to be the romantic evening that she had promised him.

Eventually, and out of impulse, he telephoned the Imperial Hotel and asked for Buller. "What now?" demanded a terse Elspeth. "I just want to talk to John," replied Mitcham. Buller came to the telephone. "Well, Graham what is it?" he demanded crossly. "I just want to inform you that the partners and I have been in your house and found a lot of the firm's files in the wardrobes in your bedroom. We have removed them." Mitcham heard Buller gasp. "You have done what?" shouted Buller. "You have no right to go into my house." Recoiling from the anger in Buller's voice, Mitcham coldly replied, "It is not your house, John. It is my house now. You transferred it to me yesterday, remember?" Buller slammed the telephone down on to its cradle. "That bloody, confounded man," he fumed to Elspeth. He

171

sat down glumly in his armchair, staring out to sea. He realised that the game was up. Mitcham had all the evidence he needed to prove Buller's wrongdoing. 'What will he do with it?' he wondered.

At that moment, the telephone rang in his room. He hesitated to pick it up. After a few seconds, he picked the receiver up to find his daughter on the line. She was hysterical. "Dad. I met Graham at our house when I got home. He was saying horrible things about you. He said that you are a thief, that you have been stealing clients' money for twenty years. I cannot believe it. Say that it is not true." Sobbing hysterically, she added, "I cannot believe that he could say such things about you."

Buller, shocked by her words, sought immediately to comfort her. "Of course, it is not true," he assured her. "How dare he insinuate such accusations against me? It is true that we had a row yesterday, such a row in fact that I dissolved our partnership. But what he has told you is despicable," he lied. "Dad, I am so glad that you told me that. I never doubted you for a second. But how could Graham stoop so low? I cannot believe him! I really cannot." Then, as an afterthought, she added, "I will not, I cannot marry him. In fact, I hate him. I really hate him for saying such untrue things about you." Having said that she broke down again, sobbing. Buller sympathised with her, but made no attempt to change her mind. He never wished to see Mitcham again. Replacing the receiver, he thought things through. His only ace was Susan. Would Mitcham report him to the Law

Society or, worse still, the Police if it meant losing Susan? On the other hand, he never wanted to see the man again. A fine balance, he concluded.

Susan was distraught. That Graham, a man whom she had loved, to whom she wanted to be married, could levy such horrible, untrue accusations against her father was unbelievable. She could not believe it of him. Revulsion swept through her. She ran up the stairs, into her bedroom and snatched her photograph of Mitcham out of its frame and tore it into shreds before throwing the shreds down the toilet. Flushing the toilet and seeing the shreds disappear gave her some comfort. She pulled off her engagement ring and threw it hard against the wall. "I do not want to see him again," she screamed uncontrollably. With that she threw herself on to her bed, sobbing hysterically.

Mitcham felt bereft. Deflated, he poured himself another whisky. 'I do not know how I am going to get through all this,' he reflected. It seemed to him that he had lost everything: his love and marriage, his reputation, his solvency, his career and his firm. 'Nothing much else to lose,' he told himself sorrowfully.

His father listened sympathetically to Mitcham as he described the events of the day, and the consequent effect on Susan. The breakdown in his son's engagement was not a surprise to him, indeed he had expected it to follow his son's discovery of her father's fraudulent misbehaviour. 'How could it be otherwise?' he had reasoned. For her fiancé to be the discoverer and exposer of her father's career of fraud could only have one conclusion. The termination of their engagement, the cancellation of their wedding plans. "Heaven knows what would have happened if this had all come to light after the wedding," he had remarked to his wife when they were discussing the scandal earlier in the day. But what had come as a complete surprise was the revelation that all the files relating to the frauds were stored in Buller's bedroom wardrobes. 'How on earth do you sleep with evidence of your crimes all around you?' he wondered. He also wondered how long it would take for his son to repay the loan of £20,000 which he was due to make to him on the Tuesday. "You have behaved impeccably throughout," he reassured his son. "I am so glad that you reported Buller to the Law Society. Doing so certainly puts you in the clear."

This last point had not occurred to Mitcham, so preoccupied had he been in establishing the truth, and the scale of the firm's deficit. The remark came as a bit of a shock to him. It had never occurred to him that his own conduct could be questioned.

"And when the whole wretched business has been sorted out," his father continued, "Susan may well come to realise that you had no alternative than to act as you did, even if it meant destroying the most important thing in your life, your relationship with her. Time is a great healer, you know."

His wife, who had been listening intently to her husband's end of the conversation, nodded her head affirmatively. Grabbing the telephone, she told Mitcham to stand firm to his principles, take everything steadily, and in due course everything would sort itself out. Most of all he was not to stress himself too much, but to try to keep as detached an emotional distance to the unravelling of the drama as he could. Thanking them, Mitcham felt more confident and determined to see the whole wretched nightmare through.

The telephone rang. Mitcham looked at it dispassionately. Was it Susan? Or Buller? Or Howard?

He lifted the receiver. It was Elspeth. "Graham. John has gone down to the bar, so I am free to talk. I think that you ought to know that Susan telephoned John earlier this evening. She was hysterical, telling him that you had accused him of being a thief, and of stealing money from clients for twenty years. John denied the accusations, although he admitted that he had had a row with you on Friday, and that he had dissolved the partnership. Graham, he is in denial." Mitcham listened to this in horror. "Graham, you must believe me that I knew nothing of what John was up to. I really did not. His behaviour has been disgraceful. I wanted to go home yesterday, but he insisted on staying here until Sunday. And he still keeps on talking about us getting married! By the way, have you told the Police?" Mitcham assured her that he had not done so, but that he had reported the

breaches of Solicitors' Accounts Rules to the Law
Society. "I understand, Graham. You clearly had no
alternative." Mitcham enquired as to what their
movements were likely to be the following day.
"John insists on staying here for lunch, and driving
home after lunch. You will not tell him about this
conversation, will you, Graham? Please!" Mitcham
assured her that he would not. He then asked her
when Susan was likely to return to London to work.
Tomorrow or Monday morning? Elspeth did not
know, but thought that Susan would want to see her
father before returning to London.

Sunday 16th May 1982

Susan woke from a troubled sleep. She was angry
and distressed. Angry with Mitcham that he had
impugned the integrity of her father. Distressed that
his behaviour, so despicable, had caused her to break
off their engagement, with the consequential
cancellation of their wedding. His callous behaviour
towards her father made it impossible for her to marry
him. But the shock led to a sense of bereavement, a
numbness of love feelings, a love that was in denial.
She hated him, and yet the chemistry of love was not
banished – it was still there, but diminished. The
previous night she had wept and wept at her loss, and
her humiliation. She resolved to delay her departure
for London until she had seen her father. She had to
tell him how much she loved him, how much he
meant to her, and how distressed she was by

176

Mitcham's unwarranted accusations. But, besides this resolve, she wept and continued to weep at her tragic circumstance. To love a man one moment, only to hate him the next, was unendurable. She sought solace from her hen party friends, who were astounded by her tragic revelation. In turn, they poured sympathy and consolation on Susan. For Susan anger, deep regret and heartache proved a vicious cocktail, which lasted the whole day.

Mitcham, Howard and the three junior partners were at the office early on Sunday morning. Howard had already set up the firm's accounts on a computer stationed on a side table. Piled on the Board Room table were three suitcases and several black bags. They opened each suitcase and emptied the files on to the table top. They then listed each one in alphabetical order in a notebook. They then double checked the list against the files to ensure that there were no omissions, and Mitcham then inserted the date and time of the compilation. Then they turned their attention to the tedious task of emptying and sorting the contents of the black bags. These papers were divided into separate piles; personal, clients, accounts/financial. Once completed, each pile was arranged in chronological order. Then each item was given a number, and entered into a separate notebook, which was then dated and timed. Satisfied that the audit was complete, the partners and Howard sat around the table in complete silence reading the contents of each file and correspondence. Each breach of Solicitors' Accounts Rules was noted. Howard traced each transgression on the relevant client account; and a brief note was made of the nature and form of each offence in a third notebook.

At 11 am. Mitcham telephoned the Imperial Hotel and asked to be put through to Mr. Buller. After a few minutes had passed, Buller came to the phone: "What do you want now?" he demanded grumpily. "John, I want you to be at the office at 8 a.m. tomorrow to hand over your office keys and to collect any personal belongings that you have in your room. After that, you are not to step inside the office again except with a written authority signed by me, or at my invitation. Is that understood?" A series of grunts could be heard coming from the other end of the telephone. "And on Friday afternoon I notified the Law Society that you had committed breaches of Solicitors' Accounts Rules." "You have done what?" roared Buller from the other end. "I had no choice, John. In fact, the partners, Howard and I are in the Board Room at the moment reading through the firm's files and correspondence which we found in your bedroom yesterday afternoon, and it is quite clear that you have been committing acts of fraud for a very long time. I will see you at the office tomorrow at 8 am." To a response of spluttered expletives, Mitcham replaced the receiver in its cradle.

Late in the afternoon, the partners and Howard finally finished their reading of Buller's files and correspondence, and completed their annotation of his crimes. A discussion ensued. They agreed that his crimes fell into three categories: transferring clients' money by cheque straight out of a client's account into his private Bank account at the Assurance Bank; borrowing money from various Banks by giving an undertaking on firm notepaper to repay the loan with interest on the completion of a fictitious deal; by stealing monies from estates of deceased persons where he was the sole executor and issuing false estate accounts to cover his thefts. The correspondence found in his bedroom was mainly with the Assurance Bank and revealed that the Bank had been prepared to lend him money on the expectation that the loans would be repaid with clients' money. Buller had in effect been conducting a separate book of accounts with clients' money, unbeknown to his partners, Howard, the firm's accountants, or the Law Society.

There was also correspondence from disgruntled clients demanding to know when they would receive their money, letters from the Law Society in response to complaints made to them by clients seeking payment of monies due to them and not paid. Mitcham was amazed that clients had never complained to him about any of these matters. The firm's Complaints Procedure issued to every client at inception of instructions informed clients that, if they had a complaint about Mr Buller's work, they should refer their complaint in the first instance to Mr. Mitcham, or failing him to another partner of the firm. 'And yet this has not happened, presumably because Buller was the Senior Partner,' mused

179

Mitcham.

There were even instances of letters of complaint
from other firms of solicitors to whom exasperated
clients had gone for help. And there were letters from
other Banks seeking repayment of loans secured by
undertakings given on the firm's notepaper by Buller.
'Oh! I wish that I had not left it to him to open the
post in the mornings!' Mitcham reflected peevishly.

It was clear that the scale of his misappropriations
had reached such a size that Buller was no longer in
control of it. It was only a matter of time before the
whole rotten business would come crumbling down.
'No wonder that he rarely took a holiday,' thought
Mitcham, 'and even when he did it invariably was
only for a week at a time. He simply had to be in the
office to prevent the frauds from being revealed.
What a strain it must have been for him!'

The partners analysed the legal implications of what
they had discovered, and considered the various
courses of action open to them. Amanda asked
whether the firm's professional indemnity insurance
would cover losses to clients; a suggestion that had
not occurred to Mitcham. It was agreed that on
Monday Mitcham would contact the insurers and
report the losses with a view to making a claim if this
were possible. They discussed whether their findings
should be reported to the Police, but decided to defer
that decision until they had learned the view of the
Law Society.

Mitcham warned his partners that he was apprehensive that, if the news of Buller's frauds became public, there would be a run on the firm's bank accounts by both the firm's creditors and by clients and that he wanted the matter played down. He did not wish it to be said that Buller had transferred clients' money into his private bank account, and suggested that clients should simply be told that Buller had retired from the partnership. If clients pressed for more information, then they should be told that Buller had committed breaches of the Partnership Agreement. This would not suggest that he had defaulted with clients' money, and should be readily accepted as a sufficient reason for his leaving the partnership. This line of approach was agreed. Howard then reported on the firm's cash flow position and they agreed that it was manageable without the need for redundancies

----

Yet despite all the evidence that he had unearthed, Mitcham was still struggling with the fact that Buller, so kind and supportive, so gentlemanly, had been capable of fraud, of lying and deceit, and on such a scale. It was difficult to believe. This was not the case with Susan. It had been such a shock to her that Mitcham should accuse her father of fraud, that she could only see malevolence on his part. She did not reason why he should make such an accusation, it was enough that he had done so.

Buller walked slowly up the driveway to his front door. He had escorted Elspeth to her home, told her that he loved her and kissed her goodnight. Now he had to convince his daughter that he had done nothing dishonourable, a task for which he had no appetite. He had already decided that he would seek to divert her attention from the issue of his alleged wrongdoing by discussing the future of her relationship with Mitcham. At least that would occupy a lot of her concentration and time.

The front door swung open to reveal a distressed, tear stained Susan standing before him. She stumbled crying into his arms, and held him limply in her arms. "Oh, Susan. What can I say to comfort you?" he consoled. He led her gently into the living room, and sat her down on the sofa. "I am so sorry, Susan, that my disagreeable row with Graham on Friday has caused you such upset," he comforted her. "I have dissolved my partnership with him because it is clear that mutual trust between us has gone, but this is no cause for you two not to marry," he soothed, confident that this was no longer a possibility.

"But he has accused you of stealing money from clients, which you deny. Of course, you have not. You would not dream of doing anything like that. It is despicable of him to make such malicious accusations. It is just a smokescreen to get out of marrying me. I never want to see him again." With those words she broke into tears, and sobbed whilst Buller cringed. He put his arm around her gently, and held her for some time, realising the suffering that he had caused to the person who mattered most to him, his daughter. As her tears subsided, he told her that he was going to meet Mitcham at 8 o'clock in the morning to sort matters out and to remove his personal belongings. This announcement caused Susan further anguish, and Buller settled down to a long evening of remorse.

Neither Susan nor Buller could sleep that night. Susan felt bereaved, and was worried about her father. For him to be talking about setting up a new Solicitor's firm on his own was, she knew, a considerable challenge for a man of his age. He had talked to her quite bullishly during the evening of his prospects and plans. She had tried to persuade him that now was the time for him to retire, but he had insisted that he enjoyed the law and work too much to consider retirement. Assuming that he could find suitable office premises, he thought that he could be operational within two months, and that in the meantime he would contact his clients and continue his practice from home.

Buller realised that the time of reckoning was fast approaching. He had bluffed Susan that evening, quite deliberately. He could not face the humiliation of admitting his crimes to his adoring daughter, and had enjoyed the fiction of discussing and planning his new career with her. He was not at all certain that he could endure the revelation of his crimes to his daughter. He certainly did not want to be present when she learned of his frauds.

His thoughts turned to Elspeth, who had been evasive whenever he mentioned marriage. Would she stand by him whilst he endured the ignominy of being struck off the Roll of Solicitors, which he knew would now be inevitable. Worse still was the possibility of being arrested by the Police for fraud, with the inevitable prospect of trial at the Crown Court and prison. He shuddered. "How would that come about?" he reasoned. He doubted that Mitcham would report him to the Police. This would shatter any hopes that Mitcham might still harbour of marrying Susan. If it came about at all, he thought that it would be the Law Society who would report him to the Police.

The tension built up inside him: electric spikes pulsed through his nervous system and his stomach nerves felt taut. He noticed that his hands were shaking. He tried to distract himself by reflecting on his financial position. If Elspeth would marry him, then they could survive on their joint pensions and her savings. But if she left him, or refused to marry him, then a future of penury faced him. His pension would at best feed and house him, little more. Whichever way he directed his thoughts they all returned to the desperation of his plight. He felt sick.

Elspeth meanwhile felt drained. The week's holiday

with Buller, to which she had looked forward so much, which had promised peace and relaxation with the man she loved in the hotel that had played such an important, romantic role in her life, had been rudely shattered. Her hope that by the end of the week Buller would have proposed marriage to her had indeed been fulfilled, but the basis for his proposal had been changed by the shock of the revelations of his fraudulent behaviour which had emerged so violently during the week. It was not borne out of love for her, but out of an urgent need for her financial support for his future. Was she no more than just another victim of his greed? Both of them had spent their respective honeymoons at the Imperial Hotel, it was a special place for both of them, a hotel where she had hoped they would both spend their joint second honeymoons. But not now. The idyll had been sullied by the horrible events of the week. She felt bewildered by the sudden turn of events, and confused. Mitcham had advised her to ditch him. Was he right? Was that really what she should do? Torn by indecision, worried about her future, and apprehensive about her feelings for Buller and how she should relate to him in the future, she prepared herself for bed. Perhaps sleep would provide the answer.

CHAPTER FOURTEEN

Buller had not been able to sleep. Stomach nerves
had prevented him from sleeping. He felt wretched.
The tension was unbearable. He had never imagined
that his guilty secret life would unravel so
traumatically and, once discovered, so quickly. He
had always assumed that he would be able to control
events, and that one day he would be able to pay off
the debt that he had accrued through his
misappropriations. To find his frauds exposed by his
prospective son-in-law, and to have to lie to his
daughter to conceal his guilt, yet knowing that it
would only be a matter of time before his guilt would
be revealed to his daughter, was a pincer from which
there was no escape. His pain was excruciating. He
tried to turn his mind to his forthcoming meeting with
Mitcham. Would he be able to limit any further
damage, to dissuade Mitcham from reporting the
matter to the Police? But he felt paralysed with fear
and foreboding. He could not formulate coherent
thoughts. All he could foresee was a tense meeting
with a terse, unsympathetic Mitcham. He dreaded the
prospect of pleading with Mitcham not to report him
to the Police, of warning him that Susan would not
forgive him if he were to do so, that his prospect of
marrying her would be irremediably damaged if he
did so. He cringed. What was he to do? He tossed
and turned in bed, unable to settle. He could not
believe that he had been such a fool not to realise the
inevitability of the crisis that lay before him. Why?
Why had he been so stupid, so naïve, so callow?
Why had he chosen to follow a path that could only

lead to the devastation of everything that mattered to him – his relationship with his daughter, his career, his status and position as a senior partner of a distinguished, albeit small, firm of solicitors, his home and his earnings. His dismissal from the partnership, and Elspeth's rejection of his offer of marriage, symbolised the disaster of what was to befall him. Tears welled up in his eyes and for a while he wept, his body shaking uncontrollably as self-pity and fear dominated his mind, and nausea gripped his body. He wanted to escape his ordeal, to turn the clock back, to pretend that none of this had happened, that he had done it all with the best of intentions, to provide for his family, to buy a house for them, to build up capital within the firm by not drawing out his full share of profits, but he knew that nothing justified what he had done. Shame and ignominy dominated his thoughts. He knew that that was the reality. He was doomed. He had failed. At last he succumbed to a fitful sleep, dominated by nightmares of horrors to come.

Monday 17th May 1982

Buller arose haggard and tired. He had a hot bath, and shaved, but found that he was unable to look at himself in the mirror. He was ashamed of himself. He was a bag of nerves. In his kitchen, he made himself a slice of toast, but found that he could not eat it. A cup of coffee brought no respite. He could not endure the thought of attending the meeting with

Mitcham. If only he could escape the ordeal which
lay before him. On an impulse, he scribbled a note to
Susan, and left it on the kitchen table where he knew
that she would discover it. Quietly he let himself out
of the house. Once in his car he started the engine
and reversed slowly out into the road. He set a course
away from Menston, away from the office, away from
responsibility, away from reality.

Susan arose at 7 o'clock. She had not slept well, but
was determined to see her father at breakfast before
he left for his meeting with Mitcham and to wish him
luck. Dressed in a dressing gown she descended the
stairs and entered the kitchen. She saw a partly eaten
slice of toast on the table, and a partially empty cup of
coffee. Her father had obviously risen early. And
then she saw the note that her father had left for her.
She read it. At first, she was uncertain what it meant,
until it dawned on her with increasing horror that he
was contemplating, indeed intending to commit,
suicide. Panic struck her. Numbed by horror, she felt
her limbs shake as she read, and read again, the
message that her father had written to her in his note.
The message seemed clear. He was going to kill
himself. Screaming she ran up the stairs to his
bedroom, but he was not there. In a frenzy, she ran
down the stairs and out on to the drive. She ran to the
garage and opened the garage door, but his car had
gone. She retreated into the kitchen, and trembling
read, and then studied, his note. It still seemed clear
to her that it was a suicide note. She tried to compose

188

herself, and then, on impulse, she telephoned the Police.

At 7.30 am. Mitcham picked up the crate containing six milk bottles standing outside the office front door, whilst Howard unlocked the door and switched off the security system. Mitcham took the milk to the kitchenette, and made two cups of coffee. He and Howard then took their places in the office reception waiting for Buller's arrival. Conversation was desultory. Both felt tense. As 8 o'clock came and passed, both grew tenser. Five minutes later the tension was broken by the office telephone suddenly ringing. Mitcham picked up the receiver and cautiously said, "Mitcham of Buller & Mitcham. Can I help you?" "P.C. Percival of Menston Police here," replied the caller. "Were you expecting to meet Mr. Buller at 8 o'clock this morning?" "Yes," answered Mitcham. "And has he arrived?" "No," replied Mitcham. "Why?"

"His daughter has telephoned us to report that her father had left home to attend a meeting with you at your office at 8 o'clock, but that after he left the house she found a letter addressed to her which read like a suicide note. We have mounted a search for him. Do you know of any of his favourite haunts?" Mitcham confessed that, apart from Salcombe in Devon, he did not know of any. He told them Elspeth's address, but Susan had already told them that. "If he should come to your office could you telephone us immediately,

189

please, so that we can stand down the search." With that request, P.C. Percival rang off. Mitcham told Howard what he had been told.

Mitcham felt terribly emotional for Susan, imagining her state of mind, and wishing desperately that he could console her. He longed to telephone her but he did not know whether to do so would not cause more damage to her and to their relationship. If their relationship were to have a future, passage of time would heal it. But he knew what lay ahead for Buller; he would be struck off the Roll of Solicitors, he would be made bankrupt, and, almost certainly, be prosecuted for fraud, tried before the Crown Court, and sent to prison. He would be totally humiliated. Susan would have to assist and comfort her father through this succession of ordeals, all of which were triggered by Mitcham. And certainly, at least in the early stages of this process, she would lay the blame on Mitcham, attributing false motives to him. For him to approach her now offering sympathy and comfort would be nauseating for her, and he would be made to feel a complete creep. Best to leave a wounded animal alone, he reasoned. Time might heal.

An hour later his telephone rang. "Reverend Paterson of Saint Swithun's Parish Church here," a self-assured voice said. "I am comforting Miss Susan Buller, who is with me, and has told me that her father appears to be missing and she is frightened that he has committed, or may be contemplating committing, suicide. I understand that he was due to meet you at 8 o'clock this morning but did not turn up. Is that correct?" Mitcham confirmed that Buller had failed to turn up for his meeting and was not in the office. "Do you know of any place where he was likely to go?" was the next question. Mitcham was unable to help, but seized the opportunity to ask the vicar to pass his commiserations on to Susan and to tell her that, so far as legal etiquette allowed him to do so, he would always be ready to talk to her if and whenever she wanted to do so. Reverend Paterson agreed to do so, and then added words that were to haunt Mitcham for the rest of his life: "Miss Buller has already cancelled the wedding. Oh! And the wedding reception." A bit more whispering followed, and then the vicar added: "Miss Buller has instructed me to tell you that she has informed all her family and her guests that the wedding is cancelled, and leaves it to you to notify your family and guests and the Eden au Lac. She will also cancel the flowers, the taxis and the photographer." Mitcham gazed miserably out of his office window as he limply replaced the receiver in its cradle. "Thank you, John," he muttered bitterly.

At 10 o'clock, Mitcham telephoned his firm's professional insurers to notify them of his firm's claim for indemnity to cover losses on client account. He told the executive of the happenings and discoveries of the previous few days, and was told that a claim form would be sent to him for him to complete. A little later, a Mr King telephoned Mitcham to introduce himself as a solicitor acting for his firm's insurers, and to take full details of what had happened. He instructed Mitcham to dismiss his firm's accountants and to appoint a top firm of City accountants in their place to examine the firm's client accounts and to do an audit trail of the frauds that had been discovered and to see if there were any more frauds that had not to date been identified. Mitcham agreed to do so. At the end of the conversation King told Mitcham that he had to report the frauds committed by Buller to the Police; otherwise Mitcham would be at risk of being arrested himself for being an accomplice. This suggestion shook Mitcham rigid. It had not occurred to him that the authorities would question his conduct and motives, and that they might perceive him to be an accomplice.

Mitcham swiftly summoned his partners and Howard to a meeting in his room, and reported what King had told him. They all agreed that Mitcham should report Buller's misconduct to the Police and at once. With a heavy heart Mitcham telephoned Menston Police Station to report a crime, and was put through to Detective Inspector Graves. Hesitantly Mitcham said, "I am afraid that I must report that Mr Buller, who until last Friday was senior partner of this firm, has misappropriated money belonging to clients for his own use." A sharp intake of breath indicated that Detective Inspector Graves was taken off guard. "I will be around very shortly," he announced.

Fifteen minutes later, Detective Inspector Graves, accompanied by Detective Sergeant Holden, was seated in Mitcham's office, listening incredulously to

the story of Buller's misbehaviour. When he had
finished, Graves said that he and his Sergeant had
better look at the evidence. Mitcham escorted them
to the Board Room where the files and letters found
in Buller's bedroom were set out. Howard, who had
been warned of the impending visit, was called to the
Board Room and produced printouts of the relevant
client accounts. Graves and Holden sat down to a
morning of reading.

Buller did not know what to do. The one decision
that he had made was that he was not going to
humiliate himself by going to the office and keeping
his appointment with Mitcham. "Damn Mitcham," he
muttered under his breath. "Damn him, damn him!"
But he did not know what to do. He just drove
aimlessly around, his mind awash with self-pity, self-
loathing, guilt and fear. A carousel of different
emotions, each struggling to dominate a severely
wounded conscience. He drove, and he drove.

Susan did not know what to do. She had been to see
the vicar of Menston Parish Church in case her father
had been to see him. She had telephoned Elspeth to
warn her that she thought that her father was going to
kill himself, but Elspeth had not heard from him
either. Susan was supposed to return to work at 4 pm.
that day, but she could not bring herself to do so. She
loved her father, she had to be with him, to nurture

him through his trauma, to tell him how much she loved him, to beseech him never to harm himself, to remind him that one day she would make him a grandfather of her children, a grandfather to be loved and cherished. She could not go, to leave him alone to a grisly, solitary death She had to be there, at home, to find out what had happened to him, to bring him solace and comfort if he were still alive, to make arrangements for him if he were dead. The very thought that he may be dead made her scream in agony. She realised that she was in no fit state to return to work; in fact, she could not, she had to be at home, to be with her father.

At 4 o'clock in the afternoon there was a knock on Mitcham's office door. Detective Inspector Graves poked his head round the door. "I have just heard from P.C. Percival that Mr. Buller has been found alive and well," he announced. "Can I come in?" Mitcham beckoned him to a chair. Graves closed the door and sat down. "Apparently, Buller called on a lady friend called Elspeth Shaw about an hour ago, and she telephoned P.C. Percival with the news. P.C. Percival has telephoned Mr. Buller's daughter, a Miss Susan Buller, to tell her the good news, and has asked me to tell you. I understand that you and Miss Buller know each other?" Mitcham nodded affirmatively, if sadly. "Now. Detective Sergeant Holden and I have read through the files in your Board Room, and we are satisfied that there is sufficient evidence to bring charges against Mr. Buller. It has left us with a dilemma though. We need to search his house before Mr. Buller has the chance to destroy any evidence that may still be in the house. We need to get a search warrant. We have therefore decided to arrest him as soon as he returns to his house and bring him to the Menston Police Station. That will give us time to get organised." Mitcham nodded. 'Poor Susan,' Mitcham thought. Almost certainly she will be present when the police arrest her father. What a miserable outcome! "I understand," he said slowly, dispassionately.

Elspeth had told Buller over a cup of tea that they had all been worried about him, fearful that he might commit suicide, and that Susan had asked the police to look for him. So, it was no surprise to Buller to see a police car parked near his house when at nearly 6 o'clock he returned home. He thought about approaching the car, but decided against doing so. Instead he parked his car in the driveway and walked up to his front door. He unlocked it and slowly entered. Susan was standing in the hall, her eyes red and swollen from crying. She ran towards him and threw her arms around him, wailing and sobbing as she did so. They stood for some time, locked in an embrace until Susan's sobbing subsided.

Suddenly the front door bell rang, making them both jump. Buller detached himself from Susan and opened the door. "Mr. Buller?" asked a tall, well-built man in a shabby grey suit. "Yes," replied

195

Buller. "I am Detective Inspector Graves and this is
Detective Sergeant Holden. May we please come
in?" Taken aback, Buller stood back to allow the two
men to step into the hall. "Good evening, Miss."
Graves had noticed Susan leaning limply against the
wall. "Are you Mr. John Buller, formerly senior
partner of the firm of solicitors called Buller and
Mitcham?" "Why? Yes," replied Buller uncertainly
as if in a dream. "I am here to arrest you. I have
strong grounds for believing that you have committed
fraud against clients of your firm. I want you to come
down to the Police Station for questioning. I must
warn you that you are now under arrest, and that
anything you say will be taken down in evidence and
may be used in Court against you. Do you
understand?"

Buller felt his knees buckle, as Detective Sergeant
Holden seized his left wrist and snapped a handcuff
on, then seized his right wrist and snapped the other
cuff on. Susan gasped in horror, and slid to the floor
where she lay prone, sobbing quietly. Graves knelt
by her side until she revived, and then gently eased
her into a sitting position. When, at last, Susan was
able to stand up, he led her into the lounge and guided
her to an armchair. Holden produced a glass of water,
which she readily sipped. "I am sorry, Miss Buller
but I have no alternative but to arrest your father. I
do hope that you understand," Graves said gently.
"Will you be all right on your own? Or shall I send
someone around?" Susan replied that that would not
be necessary, and rose from her armchair and walked
over to her father, who was standing nonplussed in

the hall. Kissing him gently on the cheek, she whispered, "Be strong. I love you. Always remember that." Her father nodded. "I am so sorry to have let you down, Susan," he murmured. Stiffly he turned around, and allowed himself to be ushered out of his house, down the driveway and into the waiting police car.

The arrest of her father shook Susan to the core. It had never occurred to her that this would happen. To see her father arrested and led off in handcuffs was unbelievable. It was impossible to believe, but it had happened and before her own eyes. She sought refuge in her armchair, feeling numb with shock. After a period of anguish, she recovered. What should she do? She should do something to help her father. But what? She decided to telephone a solicitor whom she knew, and who specialised in criminal law. An astonished Julian Taylor listened to the extraordinary story that Susan told him. At the end of her story he told her to leave the matter with him. He would contact Detective Inspector Graves and tell him not to interview her father until he had had a chance to talk to his client and in any event not to do so without him being present at all times. Susan thanked him. Feeling relieved that she had done something positive to help her father, Susan telephoned Elspeth to tell her of her father's arrest. Elspeth was dismayed. "But Graham promised me that he would not report your father to the police," she blurted out. "Damn the man!" exclaimed Susan savagely. "I will come round to you at once so that we can discuss matters," Elspeth volunteered.

Buller, flanked by Graves and Holden, had spent an uncomfortable twenty minutes in the back of the police car as it sped from his home towards Menston Police Station. Nothing was said throughout the journey. The handcuffs bit into his wrists. On arrival, he was unceremoniously bundled out of the police car into the charging room. There his handcuffs were removed and he was required to empty his pockets. He was then meticulously searched. His personal details were recorded in a log, and his finger prints taken. He was then escorted to the entrance to a corridor. The steel gate barring the entrance was unlocked, and he was pressed through into the corridor. The police officer escorted him along the corridor, selected a cell and unlocked it. He ushered Buller inside, switched on a low light, and then left him, locking the cell door behind him. Buller looked round the cell in a daze. 'So, it has come to this,' he thought.

CHAPTER FIFTEEN

Tuesday 18th May 1982

Mitcham opened the post next day. One item immediately caught his eye. A small, brown padded envelope addressed to him personally in Susan's unmistakeable handwriting. He looked at it with a jaundiced eye, and then feverishly tore it open. A little, sparkling object fell out. There was no letter. Mitcham picked up the engagement ring that he had given to Susan. He swallowed hard, as he gazed at the beautiful ring, which had given him and Susan such joy, and around which they had made so many exciting plans for their future together. Now it lay redundant in his hand, love cancelled, plans discarded, promises of undying love ignored. Rejection. He felt empty. He slumped in to a chair, and sat silently, mournfully considering his loss.

His thoughts were suddenly disturbed by the telephone ringing. Grabbing the receiver, he heard: "Mr. Mitcham?" "Yes," replied Mitcham. "Detective Inspector Graves here. Just a courtesy call to bring you up to date. We arrested Mr Buller at 18.15 hours yesterday and he has spent the night in the cells. His daughter engaged Mr. Julian Taylor to represent him. I have obtained a search warrant, and am proceeding to his house to search it with Detective Sergeant Holden. When we have completed that we shall interview Mr. Buller. Depending on how cooperative he is, we may then release him on bail." "Thank you for keeping me informed," replied Mitcham limply.

Although Mitcham was very used to such procedures, it was still a shock to him to be told by the Police that his erstwhile senior partner had been arrested for suspected fraud. It made him feel dirty, tarnished by association. Mitcham still found it difficult to comprehend that Buller had perpetrated fraud and on such a large scale. He could not believe that Buller would do this, even that he had the nerve to do it, for he must have realised the eventual disaster that such criminality would lead to but still he had persisted. Why? Oh, why? It was difficult to believe that in the dignified, hardworking, quiet solicitor lay such a fault line.

----

10 a.m. was approaching as Susan answered the door bell. Opening the door, she was confronted by Detective Inspector Graves, Detective Sergeant Holden and a police woman. "Miss Buller. Your father has given us permission to search this house, and we also hold a search warrant issued by a magistrate in case of difficulty. May we come in?" Susan allowed them to enter, and cursorily looked at the search warrant waved at her face. "Of course, Inspector, please carry on. Would anyone like a cup of coffee? I am just about to make one for myself." They declined. And then she added, "Is it all right for me to go into the kitchen and make one?" "W.P.C. Hughes will accompany you," replied Graves. "And is it all right if I make a phone call to my employers to explain that I shall not be in to work for a few

days?" "Yes, provided that you do so in the presence of W.P.C. Hughes," replied Graves.

It took the officers only an hour to complete their search. Mitcham and his partners had been thorough in finding files and relevant papers, and there was little left for them to discover. Nevertheless, they did find a file under a bedside cabinet in Buller's bedroom. W.P.C. Hughes searched Susan's bedroom, but found nothing of relevance. They left, thanking Susan for her forbearance.

Buller had spent an uncomfortable night in the cell. The long bench which served as a bed was hard, and the blanket which had been provided offered little warmth. From his legal experience, he knew that this ordeal was part of the softening-up process prior to the interview which awaited him, but even so it was an unpleasant experience. At 8 a.m. he was given a cooked breakfast. At 9.30 a.m. he was told that a solicitor called Mr. Taylor wanted to see him. This revelation shook Buller. He knew Julian Taylor quite well, and liked him. But he felt ashamed. To have to confess his misdeeds to a professional colleague was a step that he had not yet prepared himself for. He felt quite capable of dealing with the police interview on his own. He knew that at some stage he would have to engage a solicitor and a barrister to represent him, but by then he would have told the police what he wanted them to know. But the presence of a solicitor, and one who knew him well, meant that he

201

could not dissemble, at least if he were to keep his last vestige of self-respect. It meant that he had to tell him everything, every embarrassing fact, to confess that he had been misappropriating clients' funds for many years, that in fact he was a fraudster, a disgrace to his profession. He crumbled.

The cell door creaked open, and Julian Taylor was ushered in. The two solicitors looked at one another awkwardly. Taylor, half smiling, proffered his hand; Buller, red faced with embarrassment, involuntarily extended his hand. Hands shaken, the men disengaged. "Susan telephoned me last night to tell me of your plight, John, and to ask me to look after you. I have spoken with Graves, who has told me the gist of your problems. I understand that the police have a search warrant and are searching your house at this very minute. Then they will want to interview you. That gives us plenty of time for you to tell me all about this matter, and for us to decide what is the best course for you to follow. Shall we sit down and talk?" His quiet, confidential, comforting approach disarmed Buller. His last reservation melted away. Susan had organised this, believing it to be in his best interest. What would she think if he turned Taylor away? With a sigh, he sat down on the bench and thanked Taylor for coming to his aid. He knew that he was in safe hands with Taylor, an excellent criminal lawyer. Susan had chosen well.

CHAPTER SIXTEEN

The police interview proceeded smoothly, Buller confessed to misappropriating the monies of Miss Rudd and Miss Dixon, and of D.E. Stewart deceased. This satisfied the police for the time being. Graves said that he would wish to resume the interview after the new accountants had completed the audit trail. Buller was released on bail. Taylor gave Buller an appraising glance as they shook hands and parted. Buller walked disconsolately to the taxi rank in the Market Square.

Susan was waiting for Buller when he returned home. She saw a broken man. She rushed to him and hugged him and held him in a long embrace. When they disengaged he said, "I did it all for you. It was the only way I could afford to pay your school and university fees. The firm was not generating enough profit." Susan noted the tacit admission of guilt, and squeezed him harder. "Let's make a cup of coffee, and you can tell me all about it."

Buller was nonplussed. So much had happened to him in the past few days, particularly in the past few hours, that he was not sure what to say. His embarrassment at being arrested and handcuffed in the presence of his daughter had humiliated him to the core. To be flung into a police cell and locked in there overnight had been unendurable, in fact heart breaking. And then to find that a colleague, albeit from another firm but one whom he knew well and admired, had been called by his daughter to represent him was more than he could cope with. He broke down into tears and wept uncontrollably. Susan could not console him.

It had only been three days since she was in Paris, happy beyond belief. But in three days she had lost her fiancé, her love had turned to hate, she had said horrid words to the man she had loved, she had cancelled her own wedding, she had vilified the man she had loved, all because she assumed that he had maliciously sought to engineer her father out of their partnership by making false accusations of wrongdoing by her father. Worse still he had reported her father to the Law Society. Even worse he had reported her father to the police. She had been distressed that her father might be committing suicide. And then she had watched her father's humiliation in being arrested at his home and in her presence, handcuffed like a common criminal and being bundled into a police car to spend the night in the cells. After that, she had witnessed the police searching her home and removing a file that they had found. Finally, her father had returned to her, a broken man, who had dissolved into tears in her arms and, in as many words, had admitted that he had done wrong, and all for her. It was too much to absorb and to rationalise. All that she knew was that her father needed her support, help, comfort and solace, and instinctively she wanted to provide them, without question, without demur. Her friends, too, had been nonplussed by the traumatic change of events and had spent many hours consoling Susan on the breakdown of her engagement and discussing the underlying causes for it. But none of this had helped her. She was bereft.

Tuesday 18th May 1982

Howard poked his head round Mitcham's office door. "Your father's £20,000 has come into office account," he said brightly. "Thank God for that," Mitcham exclaimed. "At least I can carry on trading for a bit," he reflected. He still had little idea of the total amount owed to clients by Buller's misappropriations. On the credit side, he had the value of Buller's house and whatever other assets he had. The insurers may cover the frauds, subject to the deduction of his firm's excess of £12,000, and, if they did not, then the Law Society's Compensation Fund may cover the whole or part of the shortfall. It all seemed precarious to Mitcham, too much unknown, too many ifs and buts. He telephoned his father to thank him for transferring the £20,000. "How are things going?" enquired his anxious father. Mitcham told him all that he knew. "Well keep grinding away," his father encouraged him.

Later in the morning Mitcham was disturbed by a telephone call from a Mr Hardy of the People's Bank. "I understand that Mr Buller is not a partner of your firm any more, Mr Mitcham?" he asked. Mitcham affirmed. "Whilst he was a partner in your firm, some years ago he borrowed £30,000 from the People's Bank secured by an undertaking from your firm that the loan would be repaid once 5 Gordon Close, Stonely had been sold," Hardy continued. "I do not know if you are aware of this undertaking, but the Bank would like to know if the property has been sold and when it can expect the loan to be repaid." Mitcham thanked him for his telephone call and said that he would look into the matter. "I could crown Buller," he thought savagely. He wondered whether such deliberate misconduct fell within the cover of the firm's professional indemnity policy. "Only time will tell," he muttered to himself.

Wednesday 19th May 1982

The next day saw the arrival of the new accountants. Mitcham showed them the files and papers collected from Buller's house, which lay on the Board Room table, and for an hour or so explained the history of recent events. The accountants knew that their audit trail would be the basis of any criminal charges and any breaches of Solicitors' Accounts Rules that would be brought against Buller, and would quantify the amounts owed to individual clients. They set to work in the Board Room.

Mitcham meanwhile was working at a frantic pace. Not only did he have his own clients' work to do, but he had to deal with every matter concerning Buller's frauds, often at the drop of a hat, besides managing the firm and its desperate finances. On top of everything, the insurers' solicitor had required him to write a log recording in detail every single fact and happening relating to the claim, beginning with the discovery of the fraud against Miss Rudd and Miss Dixon. Mitcham found himself starting work at 5.30 o'clock in the morning in order to dictate the log, and then working at relentless speed until 10 or 11 o'clock each evening. Adrenalin kept him going, although at times he felt exhausted. He often wondered whether Susan had any inkling of what he was going through, although he knew that this was idle thinking.

Thursday 20th May 1982

"Hello, Susan. Would you and your father like to come here for lunch? I have a nice joint of beef, and I thought that you both might like to share it with me." Elspeth had not heard from Buller or Susan since her meeting with Susan on Monday evening and was anxious to know what was happening. Susan accepted the invitation. Her father had hardly eaten anything since he had left the police station, and spent his time sitting or wandering morosely around the house, wretched and dejected. To see Elspeth again and to eat his favourite meal might lift his spirits a little, she hoped. Her father was not so keen to go when she told him about the invitation, but he was in no position to refuse to go. He wanted to crawl under

207

a stone, into a hole, anywhere where he did not have to admit to his crimes, talk about them, suffer acute embarrassment and humiliation. But his daughter persisted, insisting that he put on a clean shirt, tie, smart trousers, and jacket, and have a shave. This, she hoped, might improve his morale a little.

When they arrived at Elspeth's detached cottage, Elspeth kissed Buller on the cheek, and gently guided him into her garden. There, on the patio, stood a white metal table and three chairs under a parasol. Shining on the table stood a champagne bucket with a bottle of champagne and three chilled glasses. "John, would you like to do the honours?" asked Elspeth. This request startled Buller out of his misery, and he grasped the bottle firmly in his left hand, and with his right hand he carefully removed the tin foil and wire cradle around the top of the bottle and eased the cork out of the bottle. The satisfying pop made everyone smile as John gently poured the champagne into three glasses. "Let us drink to many more occasions like this one," suggested Elspeth, and they clinked their glasses together and sat down to enjoy their champagne. "Oh, there is nothing like Moet," breathed Susan, "I could drink it every day." The conversation turned to Elspeth's garden which was looking resplendent in an array of flower beds filled with lupins, delphiniums and hollyhocks surrounding an immaculately groomed lawn. A delicious lunch followed, but any talk of Buller's misdemeanours was avoided.

After lunch, Elspeth suggested that Buller retired to

the sunbed on the lawn for a nap, whilst she and Susan cleared away the dirty plates from the table. Buller did as he was told, knowing that he would be spared the embarrassment of listening to Susan confiding the details of his arrest and charges to Elspeth. In the kitchen, Elspeth listened carefully to Susan as she detailed the events that had befallen Buller that week, her eyes closed in distress. 'What humiliation!' she thought. 'It consumes not just Buller, but Susan and me, not to mention Mitcham and his firm,' she reflected. 'How could he have done it?' she wanted to exclaim, but could not for fear of embarrassing Susan.

"And how are you coping?" she at last asked Susan. Susan broke down in tears, her body shaking with emotion. Elspeth closed in on her to hug her, and the two women stood locked in embrace until Susan's tears subsided and she was able to break free. "I can see nothing ahead for Father other than ignominy, total humiliation and prison. My biggest fear is that he will not be able to cope with it all and kill himself. At the moment he seems to be coping, but he has withdrawn into himself, and I find it difficult to read his mind. I have been able to get compassionate leave for this week, but I must return to work on Monday. I am frightened that he will wait until I have returned to work, and then kill himself. I really do not know what to do."

Elspeth looked hard at Susan, this professional woman who was used to matters of life and death in hospital, but whose emotions could not cope with the violent trauma that her father's crimes had visited on her. "And what about your engagement to Graham?" she asked. "Oh, that is off. I have terminated that, and cancelled everything and returned the ring. He has triggered all this. I hate him," Susan snapped. Elspeth recoiled, and looking hard at Susan, exclaimed, "Oh, do you not think that that is a bit harsh? He probably was compelled by events, and not able to do otherwise, don't you think?" Susan, aghast, turned on her heel, and left the room. "Oh dear!" thought Elspeth, "I have obviously said the wrong thing." She followed Susan out, caught up with her and put her arm around her. "I am so sorry to have upset you," she intoned, "I did not want to do that." Susan half turned her face to look at Elspeth, and Elspeth noticed a tear stained face. The poor girl had clearly suffered two losses and was struggling to cope. "I am here to help," Elspeth counselled involuntarily. "I will keep an eye on your father whilst you are away. You must carry on with your work. And working, you know, will restore some balance in your life, which will help you withstand the traumas that lie ahead and be a considerable comfort for your father." Susan nodded uncertainly, and squeezed Elspeth's arm. "Thank you for being such a brick," she said. They rejoined her father, and engaged in small talk until it was time to leave.

"Keep in touch," Elspeth said to both of them as they thanked her for a delicious lunch. They drove home in silence; Buller deep in thought, Susan appraising Elspeth's remark about the pressures on Mitcham. She wondered whether she had judged him wrongly.

The thought made her squirm. But she could not deny a seed of doubt.

Friday 21st May 1982

Mitcham called a partners' meeting in his room the next day. Howard was present. The purpose was to bring the partners up to date with what was happening. Mitcham told them of the fraudulent undertaking given by Buller on 5 Gordon Close, Stonely, and the conversation that he had had with the People's Bank. He had allowed himself some time to think this problem through, but was conscious that he had to reply to the Bank soon. Stephen reported that rumour was already widespread that the firm was in trouble. Mitcham advised that he had decided to take the bull by the horns and ask the insurers' solicitor whether that fraud fell within the scope of the firm's insurance policy. If it did, then he would report accordingly to the People's Bank. If it did not, then he would ask the Law Society whether the Law Society's Compensation Fund would cover the loss. If the answer were affirmative, then he would similarly report to the People's Bank. If the answer were negative, then he would ask if the Bank would accept a schedule of repayments by the firm. His partners concurred.

A little later Mitcham was on the telephone explaining the fraudulent undertaking given by Buller on 5 Gordon Close, Stonely to Mr. King, solicitor for the insurers. There was silence from Mr. King. Mitcham could hear a rustle of papers. Minutes passed. His anxiety rose. Finally, Mr King broke the silence. "I am reasonably confident that, subject to verification, this fraud does indeed fall within the terms of the policy, and you may inform the People's Bank accordingly." Mitcham's relief was palpable. He telephoned Mr. Hardy of the People's Bank, and gave him a brief synopsis of the story, and assured him that a claim would be made under the firm's insurance policy, that the firm had discussed the admissibility of the claim with their professional insurers' solicitor, and that he had advised that, subject to verification, the claim was admissible. Mitcham assured Mr Hardy that he would keep him updated. Mr. Hardy was much relieved. Mitcham informed his partners of what Mr. King had said to their evident relief, and then returned to his room. There was a spring in his step. He suddenly felt that he was winning at long last. 'Just persevere,' he told himself. He telephoned his father to tell him the good news, and then settled down to work.

CHAPTER SEVENTEEN

Days of relentless pressure and work followed for Mitcham. He was not master of his time, as accountants, insurers, police and regulators demanded his attention, distracting him from progressing his clients' cases and management of the firm. Even at the weekend Mitcham devoted all of his time to his clients' affairs, pausing only for sleep and meals. The following week dawned, and the pressures continued unabated. By the end of the week, however, the accountants had completed their audit, and identified and quantified each fraud and presented their report to the insurers and the police, and to Mitcham. It was a sizeable document. Mitcham skimmed it. He noted that the amounts stolen over twenty years, aggregated together, totalled £882,000, and that the shortfall was £232,000. He shoved it into his briefcase to study over the weekend. 'Light relief,' he thought sardonically.

Later that evening he studied the report carefully. The manner of the perpetration of each fraud was described in detail and in chronological order. Mitcham was amazed by the scale of the frauds, and marvelled incredulously that Buller possessed the cold nerve and skill to commit such fraud and on such a scale. But it was also clear that the systematic fraud had spiralled out of control and that for some months it had only been a matter of time before the whole structure would come crashing down on the hapless Buller. Buller must have known that it was out of his control, Mitcham reflected.

213

Monday 31st May 1982

Monday arrived, and at 10 o'clock Mitcham convened a partners' meeting in the Board Room, and gave each partner and Howard a copy of the accountants' report. They sat in silence, as they studied the report. The scale of the fraud was larger than any of them had anticipated. It made grim reading. When they had concluded reading, Mitcham gave them a brief update of progress with the police and insurers, and Howard reported on the financial position of the firm. When the meeting concluded, Amanda approached Mitcham and asked if she could talk to him in private. Mitcham nodded his assent, fearing that she was about to hand in her notice. That would be a body blow. She was irreplaceable.

Amanda looked pityingly at Mitcham. "I am afraid, Graham, that another fraud has come to light." Mitcham froze. "Oh, when is all this madness going to stop?" he cried out. Pulling himself together, he asked for details.

"On Friday afternoon Mr and Mrs Thornton came to see me. They told me that they were in the process of buying a guest house, and that Mr Buller was acting for them. They had paid a 10 percent deposit of £30,000 to Mr Buller and signed the contract to buy the guest house with a delayed completion date. The completion date expired a week before Mr Buller went to Salcombe. They had seen Mr. Buller that week, who had explained that there was a delay in

214

completing the purchase because the sellers had found that they were in negative equity and were unable to meet the shortfall. Consequently, their lenders were refusing to release the property from the mortgage. I thanked the Thorntons for bringing the matter to my attention, and I explained to them that Mr Buller had since left the firm and that I would investigate the matter. This morning I received a notice to complete the purchase from the sellers' solicitors. I telephoned the sellers' solicitors to ascertain the position. They told me that Mr Buller had also been acting for the sellers in the transaction and had told the sellers that the Thorntons had not been able to raise sufficient borrowing to complete their purchase. The sellers had grown weary of the delay, and then learned that Mr Buller had left the firm, so they had collected their file and instructed new solicitors to complete the transaction. After reviewing the file, they had decided to issue a notice to complete the purchase on the Thorntons. They also told me that no deposit had been handed over. I then looked at the Thorntons' client account which showed that the deposit had been paid into the Assurance Bank"

Mitcham looked impassively at Amanda as she told the story, but his calm composure concealed a. mounting anger and frustration. When Amanda had finished, he thanked her for her report and asked for the file. "What an accomplished scheming, double-faced liar Buller has been," he exclaimed. 'Perhaps I had a narrow escape when Susan terminated our engagement,' he thought ruefully

Tuesday 15th June 1982

'Dear Mr. Mitcham,

I am pleased to confirm that insurers have accepted
your firm's claims under its professional indemnity
policy as itemised in the report of your firm's
accountants as amended by the inclusion of the claim
by Mr and Mrs Thornton. The sum of £262,000 will
be paid on 15th July by bank transfer into your firm's
client Bank account. From this sum, your firm will
pay the amount due to each client, in accordance with
the draft letters appended.

Yours faithfully,

J. King'

Mitcham whooped excitedly with relief. The drama
was over. He would not go bankrupt. Clients were
going to be repaid their losses. The firm was saved.
He could not believe it. Excitedly he telephoned his
father. A relieved Mitcham senior congratulated his
son. Mitcham asked his secretary to arrange a
partners' meeting in the Board Room for 10am. and
summoned Howard to his room. A tired looking
Howard peered round his office door and was
surprised to see a jubilant Mitcham. Mitcham waved
the letter at him. Seizing the letter, Howard rapidly
read it before collapsing into an armchair. Mitcham
watched relief spread across Howard's face. Howard
remained silent for a short while as his tension, so

216

intense for so long, slowly ebbed away. Eventually a smile emerged. "Congratulations, Graham! What a relief!" he exclaimed. "I really did not believe that you would come through this," he added. "Nor did I," Graham replied. "Nor did I."

Mitcham leaned back in his chair savouring the occasion. Five weeks had passed since the first fraud had come to light, and now the crisis was over. He decided that he would take Howard and his partners out to dinner at the Falcon that evening to celebrate.

His partners shuffled dejectedly into the Board Room, apprehensive, fearing the worst, and took their customary places around the table. Mitcham and Howard were seated there, both beaming. They could not understand why. Mitcham did not waste time. He passed the letter to them, and sat back to enjoy watching their reactions.

15th July 1982

It was with excitement tinged with apprehension that Mitcham arrived at the office. The previous four weeks had been exhausting as he struggled to keep the firm together and his clients' work up to date. On receipt of Mr. King's letter he had written to all Buller's clients who were owed money by reason of Buller's frauds to inform them that his insurers had accepted liability and would be making payment on the 15th July. But until the money was in his firm's

client account he could not relax. Hours passed.
And, then, there was a knock on his office door, and a
smiling Howard entered. "The insurers' money is
in," he announced quietly. Mitcham jumped
excitedly out of his chair. "Oh, thank God!" he
exclaimed. "Now let's get that money off to the
clients straightaway. Oh, what a relief!"

Susan resumed her work schedule at St. Peter's
Hospital. Every night she telephoned her father to
check that he was all right, and to find out what he
had been doing that day, and to pass on her own
news. It was clear that he was depressed, and her
only comfort from his peremptory replies was that he
was still alive. She would then telephone Elspeth to
discuss her findings. Whenever she could she
returned home to be with her father. Months passed
in this manner.

It had not occurred to Susan, though, that an
inevitable consequence of her father's crimes was that
the insurers would seize Buller's house, her home,
and sell it to recoup part of their outlay. It was a
shock to her, when, on one weekend visit to her
home, her father, with trembling hands, showed her a
letter from the insurers' solicitors demanding vacant
possession of the house. Buller had not been
surprised to receive it, for he knew that it was
inevitable. But he had nowhere to go. Elspeth had
not accepted his overtures to marry, and had seemed
reluctant to allow him to move in with her. He

surmised that she was wary of being too closely associated with him. So, in anticipation of being evicted from his home, Buller had started to look for a house or flat with two bedrooms that he could afford to rent. But he had found none that he judged suitable or which his pension allowed.

Susan winced when she read the letter. Her home, her home since childhood, the home where her mother had died, was to be taken away from her, and sold off. She grabbed the kitchen table to steady herself, breathed deeply and stood tall. Wiping away a tear which had run down her cheek, she turned to her father and asked him what his plans were. Buller explained that he had been looking for a house or flat with two bedrooms, but had yet to find one that he liked. Susan, deciding that she had to be positive, volunteered to go around local estate agents with him that morning and to spend the weekend house hunting. At least it would give her father something to do, she reasoned, rather than moping about the house.

So, for several weekends, they house hunted together, until one Saturday afternoon an agent rang Susan to say that he had just received instructions to let a bungalow in the same road as Elspeth lived. That, thought Susan, would be ideal. The road in which Elspeth lived was in an attractive part of Menston, and it would be easier for Elspeth to keep an eye on Buller if he lived nearby. She bundled Buller into her car to meet the agent at the bungalow. The bungalow was ideal, and Buller accepted the tenancy. The next two weekends were spent packing their possessions, and deciding what furniture to install in the bungalow and what to send to auction. Buller at last had a purpose in life.

CHAPTER EIGHTEEN

December 1982

"Susan. Your father' committal is scheduled for 10 am on Monday, 6th December at Menston Magistrates Court. I do not know whether you wish to be there, but it might be sensible for you to meet him afterwards in case he needs you." Julian Taylor had kept Susan informed of the progress of her father's case, knowing of her deep concern for him. They had discussed the desirability of her attendance at the magistrates' court. Taylor had advised that it might be very humiliating for her father if she were present at the local magistrates' court. It was going to be humiliating in any event for Buller. But Susan was well known by a number of magistrates and solicitors who were likely to be in court that day. Apart from his committal to stand trial at the Crown Court, nothing further was going to happen that day. He explained that, because Buller was a well-known local solicitor, the Court authorities had already determined that the case should be heard at a Crown Court in another County, so that Buller could be assured of a fair trial if he decided to plead not guilty. Susan accepted the advice proffered by Taylor. She had no wish to be present at the magistrates' court and watch her father's embarrassment. And there was always the risk that she might bump into Mitcham at the Court, which prospect filled her with dread. She had already resolved to be at home for the weekend in order to look after her father, and to escort him to and from the Court on the Monday. To this end she had been saving up her holiday entitlement.

Buller tried to dissuade Susan from coming home that weekend. He did not want Susan to witness his humiliation in going to the magistrates' court. He dreaded the prospect himself. But to involve Susan was a humiliation too far. But Susan would have nothing of it. She was determined to be there. She had too much of her mother's stubbornness, he reflected. If she set her mind to do something, nothing would distract her. But then he was much the same, he mused.

Life had been exceedingly dull for Buller since his arrest. He had had to attend the occasional interview with the auditors as they tried to piece together the jigsaw of his frauds. He had realised early on that there was nothing to be gained by concealment of his misdoings. The auditors were too thorough and experienced to be deceived. If he proved himself to be helpful to them in their investigation and frank with the Police, then he knew that it would be taken into account by the Judge in calculating the length of his prison sentence. His guilt was clear from the facts, and he saw no advantage to himself in seeking to deny what he had done, nor the extent of his frauds. The only course for him was to do anything that might reduce the length of his prison sentence. He shuddered every time he thought of the Crown Court or prison. It was as if an electric current had shot through his nervous system. His nerves tingled,

222

his stomach nerves tautened with tension, and he would feel sick. Sharp spikes of pain would shoot up his chest wall. And there was no escape in sleep. Nightmares of standing in the dock under the withering, contemptuous glare of the Judge as he sentenced him to years of imprisonment haunted his sleep. He would wake up in a sweat to the sound of prison doors clanging behind him. He knew the sound only too well. He had attended clients in prison too many times to forget the unmistakeable clang of the metal gates, the banging shut of the prison cell door and the swirl of the keys in the lock. To try to make that experience as short as possible was his only option.

Taylor had advised him that he might secure a shorter sentence if he cooperated with the police. Together they had pored over the committal papers, and Buller was horrified when he read the total sum that he had stolen. Taylor studied his reaction whilst they read. He had no sympathy for Buller, but that was immaterial. His duty was to give him impartial advice, and that he was determined to do. But clients' reactions were always informative, and it was clear to Taylor that Buller accepted his guilt and was not going to procrastinate. Resignedly Buller pushed the papers away across Taylor's desk. "Which barrister are you going to instruct?" he enquired. "It depends on whether you intend to plead guilty or not guilty," was the reply. "Oh, guilty, of course," Buller announced resignedly. "There is no point in doing otherwise." Buller sighed. 'It is only prison. At least I am not going to hang,' he thought ruefully. "In that case I shall instruct Marcus Warren," opined Taylor. Buller nodded in agreement. He knew Warren, had engaged him himself for clients, and knew that Warren was a master of speeches in mitigation, employing a chastened tone of voice and turn of phrase, a style which was neither ingratiating nor false which irritated judges.

The weekend passed in a desultory way. On Sunday Elspeth entertained Susan and Buller to lunch. But Buller's impending visit to Menston's Magistrates' Court hung heavily in the air, dampening any attempt at jollity. "Good luck tomorrow," whispered Elspeth as she kissed Buller goodbye. "Soon it will all be over and you will be able to get on with your life," she assured him.

On the following day, Susan cooked a breakfast of fried eggs and bacon for her father, which he ate slowly and in silence. She then drove him to Menston Police Station where Buller was due to surrender his bail at 9 am. As he turned to get out of the car, Susan restrained him and gave him a kiss on the cheek. "Remember that I love you," she whispered. "Do always remember that, and that I am with you all the way." She watched him as he walked slowly to the door of the Police Station and let himself in. He did not look back.

Inside he surrendered his bail and was led to a holding cell, occupied by others, and locked in.

Furtively he looked around at the motley array of his companions. None of them appeared to recognise him, and he slouched back against the wall. An hour passed, then another, until the cell-warder suddenly unlocked the door and called out "Buller". Buller rose resignedly to his feet, and followed him out of the cell. A frisson of amused excitement greeted his entry into the courtroom, where he was ushered into the dock. Scanning the room, he recognised several lawyers, the usher and the Court clerk. But none of the magistrates was known to him, for which he felt some relief. Standing to attention he confirmed his name, address and date of birth, and then was told to sit down. He knew that from that moment he was a passenger on the journey ahead, an observer of the proceedings that were about to unfurl. He cast his eyes downwards, and listened to the prosecuting solicitor and Taylor go through the committal procedures so familiar to him. At last the ordeal came to an end and his case was committed to the Cambridge Crown Court and he was granted bail until then. He was then led back into the police station to sign the bail papers before being allowed to go. Outside the Court he found Susan waiting for him. She rushed over to him, gave him a big hug and led him by the hand to the car park where her car was parked. "Let's go home for a coffee," she said.

Months passed. Mitcham and his partners worked frantically to save the firm from an impromptu demise and to sort out the aftermath of Buller's crimes. Slowly the firm recovered, and saw new clients being introduced to it. It lost much of its probate and trust work as anxious clients removed their Wills and Trust Deeds, but other work came in to keep the firm afloat. Detective Inspector Graves had informed Mitcham that Buller had been committed to Cambridge Crown Court for trial on a date to be fixed and promised to inform Mitcham of the trial date. Mitcham felt that the end was in sight. He wondered how Susan was coping.

More months passed, and then all parties were notified of the trial date. Mitcham was warned that he was required to give evidence for the prosecution. He reported the trial date to his partners. Howard and Amanda had also received witness summonses. Mitcham dreaded the prospect of having to give evidence in court against Buller. He still found it difficult to believe that Buller had committed such crimes, so alien to his demeanour in the office. So, he felt real relief when he was told by the police that Buller, through his solicitor, had informed the Court that he intended to plead guilty and that Mitcham's attendance in Court would not be necessary. Howard asked him if he intended to attend Court anyway, but Mitcham immediately rejected the idea. He had no wish to witness the humiliation and conviction of Buller, to see him being led down the steps from the dock to start his prison sentence, nor to see the embarrassment of Susan. To be the grim reaper was not a role for him, nor one that would set him on the

226

path to winning back the love of Susan. For he was still deeply in love with Susan.

In the meantime, Susan had completed her year of duties at St. Peter's Hospital and had started her training to be a General Practitioner at Leicester City Hospital. She threw herself energetically into her new course, enjoying the spectre of qualification and the beginning of a long career as a General Practitioner. But she worried about her father, who was depressed and rudderless. She kept in touch with Elspeth in order to monitor her father's progress. Elspeth, in turn, attended Buller on almost a daily basis.

CHAPTER NINETEEN

March 1983

The long-dreaded day loomed. Buller prepared a small suitcase of clothes, shoes, and possessions to take with him into prison. Susan returned to the bungalow two days before the trial date in order to watch over her father. On the last evening, she cooked a joint of roast beef, her father's favourite dish, and the two of them sat down to eat it on the dining room table. They reminisced about happier times, as they ate and drank from a bottle of Burgundy red wine that Susan had bought. Susan sensed that her father was relieved that his ordeal was coming to a conclusion, and that he was mentally prepared for the challenge ahead. When the evening drew to a close Susan hugged her father hard for a long time, before giving him a gentle, loving kiss on his cheek.

Susan endured a restless night in bed. The next day was going to be a nightmare. She could not release herself from her dread. Tension swept through her, thoughts swirling through her mind. "Would Mitcham be there?" she suddenly wondered. The very thought caused her further anguish. If he was, how would she respond? Cut him dead? Ignore him? She knew that she would not be able to look through him, or avoid his eye. For the thousandth time, she wondered how she felt about him. She still felt that he could have done something to avert the disaster that had befallen her father, but the criminal proceedings that the police had brought, the seizure of her home by the insurers, the fact that her father had decided to plead guilty to the criminal charges, had made her realise that Mitcham had right on his side. Perhaps he had had no alternative but to behave as he had, to take the decisions that had led to the inevitable imprisonment of her father. Or was he motivated by greed, the prospect of owning the firm without the involvement of her father, without having to buy him out? This had been her initial suspicion, but the more she thought about it the less likely did it seem. There was little to be gained when after all Mitcham was poised to marry her father's only child. And yet, could he not have done something to protect her father? The unresolved thought nagged away at her. Perhaps, when the trial is over and people are free to talk, she might get an answer to these unresolved doubts? Perhaps Taylor may be able to shed some light on the subject? But even if he did where would that leave her? Her engagement to Mitcham was long gone, buried. How could it be revived in a meaningful way with her father languishing in prison? And on his release, how would Mitcham get on with her father or her father with him? There was no future in such thoughts. Besides, for all she knew Mitcham was now seeing someone else, perhaps was in love with someone else. The torment was insufferable. She could not sleep.

Susan surveyed the Court room from the public gallery with a jaundiced eye. A few members of the

229

public were scattered around her on the public benches. Huddles of clerks and barristers in whispered conversations gathered on the benches below her. The Judge's bench was empty. Policemen loitered about. Journalists yawned. And somewhere, far out of sight, was her father, a solitary figure, lost in despair at his impending humiliation and his inevitable imprisonment. Her sadness for him overwhelmed her, and tears swelled in her eyes. She tried to distract herself, but could not. She suddenly noticed Julian Taylor enter the Court room. Evidently things were going to start to happen. Spasms of tension took over her. Then she saw her father, being led in handcuffs up the steps into the dock. He seemed shrivelled, she thought.

"Silence in Court," demanded the clerk of the Court, who then turned to bow low as the Judge entered the Court room. Susan scrutinised the Judge. A hush descended on the Court. "What sort of Judge is he going to be?" she wondered; a harsh, vindictive judge, a forgiving, lenient judge or a sound, sensible one? Oh, how she wished for a forgiving, lenient judge. The Judge, resplendent in a wig and violet gown, bowed to the assembled throng, who in turn bowed to him. "Regina versus Buller," intoned the Court clerk, who, after establishing Buller's identity, proceeded to read out a list of thirty-three charges. To each one he demanded whether Buller pleaded guilty or not guilty. To each Buller, standing in the dock, pleaded guilty in a firm, resonant voice. He was conscious that all eyes were upon him, and he was determined not to show any weakness. He had rehearsed this scene in his mind and in his sleep many times in the past months. It was now second nature to him, and, despite his inward tension, he felt a confidence in speaking his plea. After all it did not require any thought on his part.

Theatrically, the prosecuting barrister rose to his feet. His role was a simple one, but he was determined to make an impression. Pompously, he set out the essential facts which constituted each offence. Two hours passed before he reached the final charge. Having dealt with that, he paused and then reminded the Judge of the gravity of the offences. The accused had broken his duty of trust, and, he declared with a flourish, had thereby sullied the reputation of the Solicitor's profession. A heavy custodial sentence was necessary to restore the public's faith in the integrity of the profession. Satisfied with his performance, he sat down and noisily gathered his papers together.

Marcus Waring then stood up to address the Judge. He reminded the Judge that his client had admitted his guilt at the earliest opportunity, actively assisting the auditors in their task, and readily admitting his guilt to the Police. This had minimised the cost of Court proceedings. He had repaid a substantial amount of the insurers' losses by the sale of his house and other assets. He then asked the Judge if he had received the probation report on Buller. "Indeed, I have," assured the Judge. "Then your Honour will know that the accused is now a bankrupt, has lost his career and his reputation. He is a contrite and broken man." Warren sat down.

The atmosphere in Court became electric. All eyes trained on the Judge. What would he do? The Judge wasted no time. He glared at Buller. "Oh dear" thought Susan. Buller flinched. "You have pleaded guilty to a host of criminal charges, stretching back some twenty years. It has been a catalogue of deceit, cold calculating deception of clients who put their trust in you to look after their money. Instead you stole it for your own benefit. The profession of a solicitor, a noble profession, has its basis in trust. Without trust the profession cannot operate. You have betrayed that trust, not just once but by your own admission thirty-three times. You have deliberately let down your clients, your colleagues, your profession and your profession's standing in the eyes of the public. It has been an absolute betrayal of the trust reposed in you. I have read your probation report, noted your remorse and the fact that you are being treated for depression. Your defence counsel has told me that you are now bankrupt, that you have lost your career and your reputation. But you were the engineer of this calamitous state of affairs. You brought it all on yourself. There is no one else to blame, just a fault line in you, a reckless disregard of trust. I have taken into account that you admitted your guilt at the earliest opportunity, but no doubt you did that hoping that it would reduce the severity of your sentence. I have to weigh that up against the length of time that you conducted these frauds, some twenty years." The Judge paused, a theatrical pause. Everyone present stiffened.

"The sentence must do three things," he announced. "It must reflect a need to punish. It must serve as a deterrent to other solicitors. It must restore the confidence of the public that such fraud by a solicitor will be severely punished." Susan groaned. "You are a disgrace to the profession. A severe sentence is required. You will serve a sentence of five years' imprisonment for each offence, each sentence to run concurrently. Take him down," he ordered, ignoring a gasp from the public gallery. Buller's face blanched and his legs buckled. It was a longer sentence than he had feared. In distress, he looked vainly around the Court, looking for Susan. "Take him down," commanded the Judge.

Susan found Julian Taylor waiting for her at the foot of the stairs leading from the public gallery. "Are you all right?" he asked sympathetically. Susan nodded miserably. "Marcus and I are going to the cells to talk to your father. Do you wish to come?" Susan nodded, and followed him down the corridor. Minutes later the three of them were being ushered through the steel gate into an interview room. A minute later Buller was ushered in. He was in abject misery. They sat down. "I am afraid that you were up before Judge Benson," sympathised Warren. "He is notorious for handing out stiff sentences. But it was within a range of sentence available to him albeit at the top end. I am not at all sure that an appeal against the length of sentence will succeed, and there

233

is always the danger that the Court of Criminal Appeal will disagree and increase the sentence. After remission for good behaviour, in today's climate of pressure on prison places, you should be free in about two years. However, I will give some thought to the prospects of an appeal, and will advise Mr Taylor in due course. It is never sensible to make decisions in the heat of the moment. Calm reflection is required." Buller nodded dejectedly. He could scarcely look at Susan, his shame complete.

After the interview was over, and Buller had been led away, Taylor invited Susan to go to a local café for a cup of coffee. Susan had hardly spoken, even to her father. A change of atmosphere might help her recover from her ordeal, Taylor reasoned. Seated, coffee ordered, Taylor studied her, a picture of distress. 'No point in talking,' he decided. 'Leave it to her to broach conversation and take it from there.' He stirred his coffee and waited. Susan sipped her coffee, slowly, steadily, until its warmth and caffeine began to revive her. "I do hope that he can stand it," she whispered. "I am sure he will," Taylor assured her. "He is of strong mettle." Susan finished her coffee with a sigh.

"What did the Judge mean when he sentenced father to five years in prison for each offence, but the sentences were to run concurrently," she muttered enquiringly. Taylor looked sympathetically at her. She had clearly not understood the effect of the word 'concurrently'. "Oh, it means that, whilst the Judge sentenced him to five years' imprisonment for each offence, the sentences will run concurrently, that is they run at the same time. So, the maximum time that your father will serve altogether is five years, no more." "Oh, I see," Susan murmured.

They lapsed into silence. "Would you like another coffee?" Taylor asked her. Susan, anxious to avoid the real world outside, to remain in the cocoon of warmth and safety of the café, nodded. As she sipped the second cup of coffee, Taylor asked her if she had any questions for him, any advice that he could give. This jolted Susan out of her remorse, and she addressed the question. Her thoughts drifted to Mitcham. "I did not see Graham Mitcham in the Court," she murmured. "Oh, he was not there," Taylor replied. "It would be the last place that he would want to be. The whole affair has been a tragedy for him." Susan blinked.

"What do you mean?" she asked quietly. Taylor was aware that Susan had been engaged to Mitcham, and that she had broken off the engagement following Mitcham's discovery of Buller's offences. He looked tenderly at Susan. "Oh, he had no choice in the matter," he demurred. "Once he had learned of the first fraud he had a duty to investigate it and to reveal it to the authorities. He would have been culpable if he did not." Susan gulped. "What do you mean?" she asked. Taylor continued, "Look, every solicitor is duty bound to expose any transgression within their firm. These were very serious offences. Do you think that Mitcham could have turned a blind eye to them? It took courage on his part to grasp the nettle, and to expose his senior partner's crimes. From what I have heard and read, it showed extraordinary leadership on his part. But if he had not displayed that, he would have been disciplined by the Law Society, and insurers would probably have refused to accept liability and pay out those clients who were defrauded. Besides his partners would not have accepted it. They would have left the firm in order to protect their own careers. The fact that they have remained loyal to Mitcham, and insurers have met every claim, shows how honourably Mitcham has behaved. He was facing ruin. Instead, he has plotted a true path, kept the trust of his partners and clients, and above all the Law Society. No mean feat. And he did it knowing that he had no choice but to risk the love of his life."

Taylor suddenly stopped. Susan squirmed. He had said more than he had intended to. He had not meant to hurt Susan, but from her fraught expression he knew that he had done so. "Oh, I am so sorry to have said all that," he confessed. "I did not mean to hurt you. You have suffered enough today without that contribution. But, if no one has told you that, it as well that you know it. Mitcham is a fine man."

It was too much for Susan. She rose abruptly from her chair and erratically careered towards the door. Outside she panicked for air, breathing in big draughts of air, and sobbing hysterically. Taylor followed her through the door, and put his arm around her, holding her close to him as her body shuddered with emotion until the tremors subsided and she rested limply in his arms. Her sobs subsided, to be replaced by gentle groaning as Susan recovered from her shock. Gently Taylor led her back into the café, and guided her to their table and into her chair. He sat down and slid his hand gently into her hand, conscious that everyone in the café was observing them. After a while Susan recovered her poise, wiped her face, and smiled at Taylor. "Thank you for telling me that," she whispered. "I have so misjudged Graham! I now realise what I have lost."

CHAPTER TWENTY

The telephone rang in Mitcham's office. Mitcham frowned. He was engaged in drafting a complicated commercial agreement and had left instructions that he was not to be disturbed. "Mr. Taylor is on the phone, asking to speak to you," the receptionist said. "Put him through, please, Jane."

"Graham. Buller got five years." Taylor announced. "Oh, and I told Susan that you had no other course open to you but to do what you did. I hope that you do not mind me telling her that." "No, of course not, Julian. I am very grateful to you that you did. How is Susan?" "Bushwhacked," replied Taylor. "She has been through the mill today." "Thank you for telling me, Julian," Mitcham signed off.

He looked distractedly through his office window. Perhaps there is a chance of reconciliation, he told himself, but it is too early to make any approach to Susan. Time will present the opportunity if there is to be one. He returned sadly to the unfinished document on his desk

----

Susan drove slowly back to Menston, her brain numbed from the shocks of the day. Her mind oscillated from the drama in the Court room to Taylor's revelation in the café. She could weep for her father and she could weep for herself. Over the months her initial hatred of Mitcham had weakened as doubt had entered her mind. But now she had to confront the ugly truth that, through blind love for her father, she had severed her engagement to the man she loved. No one else was to blame but herself and her impulsive, unreasoned reaction to Mitcham's unveiling of her father's offences. She shuddered. "Will I ever have the chance to put matters right with Graham?" she wondered. Had too much damage been done? And her father's presence, ever there, would be a constant reminder to them both of the tragedy that had severed their love. She drove steadily on, her mind and body seething with unending and conflicting emotions as she sought to grasp the scale of what had happened.

Elspeth opened the door to reveal a tear stained, desperate Susan. Gently she guided her into the lounge and sat her down. "Father got five years," Susan whispered, and then broke down in tears. "It was all so horrible, Elspeth. You can have no idea." Elspeth put her arm around her shoulder and cradled her until the sobbing stopped. Disengaging herself, Elspeth said that she would make a cup of tea for them both. In the kitchen, Elspeth paused and gripped the kitchen table. "Five years," she gasped. "Five years!" It was all worse than she had expected. 'Thank God I did not agree to marry him,' she thought. 'That would have been a huge mistake.' She pulled herself together as she listened to the quiet weeping emanating from the lounge. She busied herself in making the tea. Returning to the lounge, she placed the tray carefully on the coffee table in front of Susan and proffered her a biscuit. "Tell me all about it," she gently urged. Susan, punctuating her delivery with sobs and sighs, sadly related the day's events. "Well. I am glad that Mr Taylor told you that Graham had no alternative but to do what he did," said Elspeth when Susan had finished. "That is a relief for me as well as for you." The two women looked miserably at one another. "It is all too much to bear," wailed Susan. "I cannot bear it."

The metal gate clanged behind him, the key turned in the lock, handcuffs were slapped on to his wrists. Buller knew that freedom was behind him. He was steered into the prison van, and sat in the small cubicle assigned to him. 'At least the ordeal of the Court experience is behind me,' he told himself. It had been humiliating, but he had braced himself for that experience. The prison sentence was harsher than he had expected, but he had always known that a lengthy sentence was possible. The Judge's words were horrible to listen to, but he reasoned that they were no less than he deserved. He did not see any point in appealing against the length of the sentence. He shuddered at the very real prospect that the length of the sentence could be increased if he appealed. The whole horrible saga had come crushing to an end. All that he had to do was to survive the next two years and he would be free again. But he had hated the presence of Susan in the Court. He had not wanted her to be there, to listen to everything that would be said, to hear the Judge's crushing words. That was his real humiliation, his real punishment. He had tried to dissuade her from attending, but she had insisted on being there. Her love and care for her father had dominated her feelings, and naivety had clouded her from the very real drama of the Court room. Would she ever respect him again? Loss of a daughter's respect is unendurable for a father, a price too high to pay. Buller bowed his head in grief.

Hours passed, before the clanking of prison gates and shouts from outside announced their arrival at the prison. Buller joined a motley crew of younger prisoners who jeered at him. "A toff in here," shouted one to the derision of the others. There followed form filling, the confiscation of his suitcase of belongings, the indignity of a physical inspection of his private parts, and the enforced wearing of the prison uniform. He was then escorted to his cell, a long narrow room with a barred window in the end wall, and a double bunk from the top of which a foot dangled. "In here," directed the prison officer, and closed and locked the cell door behind him. 'Oh God!' thought Buller.

"Graham, I think that you should read this article." Miss Turvey brandished a copy of the Menston Daily Chronicle in front of him. The front page was devoted to the previous day's conviction and sentencing of Buller. The journalist had enjoyed a field day, relishing the drama of the story. Under the

241

banner headline of "Menston solicitor sent to prison for fraud" was a photograph of Buller, soberly dressed in a dark suit, accompanied by an embarrassed Susan, arriving at the Cambridge Crown Court.

Mitcham sighed as he read the graphic description of the proceedings. He had not looked forward to this day, knowing that the story would send shock waves not just through Menston but through the County. His own reputation would be tarnished by his association with Buller. The firm's reputation, so precariously restored, would be in danger. The repercussions for his firm's future rested on the public's reaction to the story. Mitcham read on, and then he groaned loudly in anguish as he read the last paragraph. "The defrauded clients of the firm of Buller & Mitcham have still not been repaid their losses as the firm's insurers have refused to accept liability."

Inside the newspaper Mitcham found the Editorial, which lambasted his firm for not meeting the losses of their defrauded clients and the profession at large for not having a contingency fund available to meet such losses. Mitcham seethed with anger. For the firm to have survived its crises only to be defamed by the local newspaper, and its entire future to be put in jeopardy by irresponsible, unscrupulous journalism, was unbearable and unforgiveable. 'Why did they not check the facts with me before rushing to print?' he cursed. Mitcham turned to his dictaphone, and furiously began to dictate a brief to Counsel, entitled

'Buller & Mitcham versus Menston Daily Chronicle. Counsel to settle Pleadings'.

Mitcham was sorely tempted to serve the writ himself on the Editor of the Menston Daily Chronicle. Even though two days had passed since the publication of the libel he was still seething with anger. But common sense prevailed. He instructed a process server to serve the writ in his place. Counsel had confirmed his view that the partners of Buller & Mitcham had been grievously libelled, and were entitled to an immediate retraction of the libel, an apology and substantial damages. Mitcham waited for retribution; 'Revenge is best served cold,' he reflected.

He did not have to wait long. "Mr. Mitcham. I have the Editor of the Menston Daily Chronicle on the line. He wishes to speak to you urgently." "Put him through, Jane," Mitcham urged his telephone receptionist, trying to suppress a rising wave of vindictiveness.

"Mr. Mitcham," the Editor stammered. "I have just read the writ and pleadings which you have served on me, and I see that the last paragraph in Tuesday's newspaper is completely wrong and untrue. I am so sorry. I should have insisted that we checked with you first before printing that paragraph." "Quite!" Mitcham replied icily. "I suggest that you publish an immediate retraction of the false allegation, explain fully to your readers that all clients who were defrauded by Mr Buller were repaid their losses, including interest and costs, in full by my firm's insurers more than a year ago, and a full apology. Counsel has drafted a suitable retraction and correction of facts and apology for publication, which, in view of your admission and apology, I will fax to you. I then suggest that you refer the writ to your solicitors to settle my firm's claim for damages as we assess the quantum of our losses flowing from the defamation." The coldness of his tone of voice was not lost on the Editor, who cringed with each word. Obsequiously he agreed to do as Mitcham demanded.

Emblazoned over the whole of the front page of that evening's publication of the Menston Daily Chronicle was the complete article of retraction, correction and apology that Mitcham had faxed to the Editor. Mitcham compared the wording with his draft to check that it was accurate. He sighed with relief. At least the record had been put straight, even if it meant repetition of an unwelcome story. 'Now to go for damages,' he resolved, relishing the prospect. 'Make the blighters suffer!' Two months later Mitcham accepted an offer from the newspaper to settle his firm's claim at five thousand pounds. Again, Mitcham and his partners had cause to celebrate at The Falcon that evening. "It is beginning to be a regular event," teased Stephen.

Buller did not appeal against his sentence. Marcus Warren sent a short, considered Opinion on the merits of an appeal, weighing up the arguments for and against lodging an appeal, finally concluding that there was no merit in making an appeal. Taylor visited Buller in prison, taking the Opinion with him. He would not be paid for the visit by the Legal Aid Board, but felt that it was incumbent on him to discuss the Opinion with Buller in person rather than just cursorily sending a copy of it to him in the post. He had felt caught up in the family's drama, and felt that he owed it to Susan to treat her father with respect and discuss the merits of the Opinion properly with Buller. He found a tired, distressed client. Clearly Buller was not coping with prison.

"I hear you're a fucking solicitor?" Buller looked up enquiringly at a well-built prisoner sporting a mean, vicious expression. "I don't like fucking solicitors," his interrogator postulated. "One stitched me up properly. Got me three years inside. I don't like fucking solicitors. I vowed that I would give a good hiding to every solicitor that I come across." He glared at Buller. Buller stiffened. He was ill prepared for this. He looked around anxiously seeking a prison warder to rescue him. But there was no one in the landing where they were. "I fucking hate you," his assailant shouted and swung a punch into Buller's ample midriff. Buller gasped as the pain from the punch knife-jacked him. Buller raised his arm to protect himself, as another punch hit him in the jaw. Buller screamed and cowered against the wall. His assailant taunted him: "Three fucking years

245

for nothing, just because he told me to plead guilty, when I hadn't done it. Three fucking years!" He kicked Buller in the groin, who fell screaming to the ground. Satisfied with his vengeance, his assailant leered at the prostrate Buller. "Tell the screws who done this to you and I will kill you," he menaced, and then sauntered off, his head down, whistling nonchalantly.

Buller lay prone for some minutes until he was discovered by a prison warder. A stretcher was summoned and he was dispatched to the medical wing. The doctor gave him an unsympathetic and cursory examination. "Nothing broken," he announced. "You will mend in good time." Buller was returned to his cell, where he lay suffering on his cell bed. "When will this hell end?" he cried out.

"Aw! Shut up bleating!" came a gruff voice from the upper bunk bed. "Who the hell do you think you are?" Buller grimaced, and tried to turn on to his side. A sharp pain from a cracked lower rib pierced his body and prevented any movement. He had no choice but to lie prone on his back. 'Oh hell!' he despaired.

Susan recovered gradually from her ordeal. She immersed herself in her G.P. Training course at Leicester City Hospital. Being away from Menston helped. Once a week she telephoned Elspeth for news. And she wrote to her father every week. At the end of the fourth week she took a day off work to drive to the prison in which her father was incarcerated for her first visit. She found the whole experience distressing and degrading. To see her father shuffle into the meeting room was heart-rending for her. He described his prison life and routine, but in a lifeless manner. He was clearly depressed. There was no stimulus in his routine, but the news that he had been assessed for a place in an open prison was encouraging. Susan resolved to write to the Prison Governor when she returned home to warn him of her father's depressed state of mind and the need for a doctor to monitor it. When, later at home, she wrote the letter she appended her medical qualifications to her signature to show that she meant business.

Weeks grew into months. Buller moved to the liberation of an Open Prison at Chisholme, not far from Menston, to spend the rest of his sentence. In the vegetable garden he found a solace, a refuge from the irritations of prison life. He had still not come to terms with his new, unwanted, lowly status, but in weeding the vegetable patch he could take pleasure in seeing the fruits of his labour and in the pretence that all was well with the world. Except that it was not. He dug viciously, as he contemplated his impoverished future following his eventual release from prison. Time was not on his side to start a new career, and he could not work out how he was going to fill his time. Nor was he at all certain that any of his friends and acquaintances in Menston and around the county would want to associate with him. Could he bear the ignominy of their contempt, their dismissal, worse still ostracism? Elspeth had not shown any inclination to marry him. Indeed, she had not visited him in prison, too ashamed of him, the whole experience too degrading for her. A measure of her love, or lack of love, he reasoned. He dismissed the idea of moving away from Menston to start a new life elsewhere. For one thing, Susan was planning to start her career as a G.P. in Menston. She was the only person who loved him, and valued him and needed him. It would be self-defeating to move away from her. No, he had to remain in Menston, and find something useful to do. But what?

CHAPTER TWENTY-ONE

1985

Two years passed. During that time Susan qualified as a General Practitioner and accepted a position with a general practice in Menston. She needed to be near to her father on his release, and she still harboured dreams of resuming her relationship with Mitcham, however distant a prospect that might be. She was still in love with him, and hoped that one day she might bump into Mitcham in Menston.

A vacancy for a part time Police Surgeon with the Menston Police Authority arose shortly after she took up her appointment as a G.P. in Menston. Susan had always been enthralled by the science of forensic medicine. The duties included attending injured road traffic victims, and being able to give them immediate medical relief and comfort. And it would give variety to the endless procession of patients through the surgery door. She applied for the post with alacrity. Her enthusiasm for the post won over the interviewing panel, and, despite her relative inexperience, the Authority decided to engage her. Susan was thrilled.

She continued to visit her father every month, hoping that her visits would raise his spirits, give him something to look forward to, ease his depression, which, she sadly noted, showed no sign of abating. She would visit him more often, but that was all that she was allowed.

Susan threw herself into her new work, finding it exhilarating and rewarding. She loved the responsibility of her roles, and the opportunity to put her medical training into practice.

For Mitcham, the period was one of unrelenting hard work. The blunder by the Menston Daily Chronicle had caused little damage to his firm, although it had brought wry derision among its more influential readers of the standard of accuracy of the reporters of the newspaper, to the chagrin and embarrassment of the Editor. The firm of Buller & Mitcham recovered slowly from its ordeal. Mitcham sued the Assurance Bank for damages for conspiring with Buller to defraud his firm's client account. His firm's accountants calculated that the firm had suffered uninsurable losses of £72,000, and the Bank readily paid that sum without admitting liability. Mitcham was able to repay the loan that he had received from his father with interest, and was pleased to see his firm's office account restored to a healthy operating balance. And the feeling of humiliation that he had keenly felt from the outset abated slowly with the passage of time.

As his life gradually returned to a more normal routine Mitcham toyed with the idea of selling his house and moving into a smaller property. He loved the house but, without Susan to share it, it was too big for him and was a constant reminder of his loss. But after much thought he decided that to remain living in it, rather than to discard it, would be a signal to Susan that he had not rejected his love for her, that he was open to a future with her. It was the only signal that he felt that he could send, and one that he hoped that she would learn about and assess. Somehow the ice had to be broken.

With her usual thoroughness Susan prepared for her father's release from prison. She spring-cleaned their bungalow, filled it with flowers, and laid the dining room table with their best linen, cutlery and wine glasses. She invited Elspeth to join them for dinner, and busied herself with arrangements for a surprise weekend holiday. She visited the local Ford dealership, and purchased a new Ford Escort for her father, which was delivered to her home the day before Buller's release. She put it in the garage overnight to keep it clean. She felt excitement and apprehension in equal measure.

The next day, she arose early, and drove the car out of the garage into the driveway, its front facing the road. Then she set off for to Chisholme Open Prison in her own car.

Buller was apprehensive about his pending release from prison. He had grown used to the monotonous routine, the shouting of orders by prison officers and

251

banter from inmates, the dull food and the security of his existence in prison. Dependence, not independence, was the routine of his existence and it had its own comfort. The challenge of life outside prison held little charm for Buller. He would have preferred to stay where he was, unknown and forgotten.

But the day for his release duly arrived and the prison system was determined to evict him from its care. His time was done. He was free to go. Dejectedly he ate his last breakfast in prison. He was escorted to the outer office where the paper work for his release was signed, and he was reunited with his suitcase and its contents. At 9 am. precisely the prison side gate opened, and he was escorted out. He looked back as the door was firmly bolted behind him. "Oh Lord!" he despaired. An excited shout disturbed him, and, looking around, he saw Susan rushing towards him, her arms outstretched in excitement. She threw her arms around him as he dropped his case to the ground. Then she slid her arm through his and guided him to her car. "Let's go and have a coffee," she said.

Excited, Susan sat opposite her morose father, and gazed at him as he sipped his coffee. "You do not know how much I have longed for this day," she said. He nodded distractedly. Susan prattled on, but she realised that it was going to be an uphill struggle to lift her father out of his depression. His mood did not change as she drove him home. She found him distant, disengaged.

Susan drove straight to their home. Buller's eyes were drawn to Elspeth's cottage as they drove past it. Then he noticed a shining blue Ford Escort in the driveway of his bungalow. "Whose is that?" he asked. "Your new car," announced Susan proudly. "What do you mean?" asked Buller. "It is my welcome home present for you," she told her doubtful father. "You do not have a car, and you will need one. Besides I live here, so it is the least that I can do." Buller grunted. "It is very kind and thoughtful of you," he replied guardedly. He climbed out of the car and studied the new car, and then turned to look at his home. "It will take me some time to adjust to this, you know," he said abstractedly. "I know," replied Susan, "but you have to start somewhere."

Buller looked at the joint of roast beef sitting on a platter in amazement. Two years of dreary prison canteen food had erased his memory of delicious home cooking. Susan offered the carving knife and fork to him. The evening had begun with two glasses of champagne each as Susan and Elspeth toasted his return to the fold. He already felt woozy, unsteady on his feet. But he was enjoying the sensations. At last, Susan noted, he was beginning to relax. Over a delicious dessert of brandy snaps and ice cream Susan announced another surprise. "In three weeks' time, we are all going to London for the weekend," she announced. "I have reserved three single bedrooms at the Waldorf Hotel in the Aldwych for Friday and Saturday nights. For the Friday night, I have booked a table at Rules in Convent Garden. For the Saturday night, I have bought seats at the Aldwych Theatre to watch Gershwin's 'Crazy for You'. I am sure you will love it. Then we will go to Simpsons in the Strand for Sunday lunch and then come home." As she recited this she studied their faces. Elspeth was already privy to the invitation, for Susan had had to check with her that she was available and prepared to go. She knew that her father loved musicals and Gershwin in particular, so in principle that should not present a problem. But she knew that he would need time to adjust to the rhythm of his newfound freedom, and had not wished to force it on to him too soon. 'Better to give him something to look forward to,' she told herself, 'and time to adjust.' But she wanted to give him some excitement, something to kick start him out of his misery and self-doubt. She relaxed when it became clear that they would both agree to go, and began to talk about it.

As Susan feared, Buller struggled to adjust to home life. He was not used to being in charge of himself and his routine. It made him feel insecure. Although he went for a walk in the nearby park once a day, he did not otherwise stray from his home. He pottered around the small back garden, but it hardly needed any attention from him. He learned to drive again, but found the whole exercise demanding. He read 'The Times' newspapers and attempted their daily crossword puzzles, generally without success. He prepared the ingredients for the evening meal, which Susan then cooked. Three weeks passed slowly by.

Susan made him select his best suit, shirt and tie for the weekend in London. Packed, they collected Elspeth from her home and drove to Menston railway station for the train journey to London.

The weekend was a moderate success. Buller appeared to enjoy the show 'Crazy for You', and tucked into his meals at Rules and Simpsons. But he quickly relapsed into depression, and Susan was forced to recognise that it would take many months of careful nursing to restore him to good mental health. Too much damage had been done to him.

For his part, Buller found himself superfluous. Even in prison, he counted. But alone in his bungalow he had no role to play, no interest to pursue, no one to talk to who did not despise him for what he had done. Even Susan's attentions were too overwhelming. He wished that she would stop trying to organise him, to organise him to do something that he did not want to do.

And he was conscious that his existence was preventing Mitcham and Susan from getting together again. How could they when he was always about, the elephant in the room.

CHAPTER TWENTY-TWO

The birds were singing, the sun was shining as Susan returned home from the surgery. She noted that the Ford Escort was not standing in the driveway where it had been in the morning when she left for work. Her father had obviously gone out for a drive, she reflected. She pulled up outside the garage doors, and climbed out. As she did so she thought that she could hear a car engine running. Looking around she could not see any car. Then, with an anguished scream, she ran to the garage door to pull it open. It would not yield. It was locked. She ran back to her car to retrieve her car keys. Selecting her garage key, she ran back to the garage door and unlocked it. Pulling it up she gasped as a wall of exhaust fumes hit her. She noticed a hose attached to the exhaust pipe running alongside the car. She ran to the driver's door, seeing her father slumped over the steering wheel, his head resting on his arms. The engine was still running. The door was locked from the inside. She pulled the hose out of the slit at the top of the window. She tried to open the internal door into the bungalow but this too was locked and the door sealed. In panic, she ran out of the garage, gasping for air. She pulled the keys out of the garage door, ran to the front door, and unlocked it. Taking the Escort car key off the key rack, she ran desperately back into the garage, unlocking the car door as she did so. Opening the door, she turned off the ignition and felt for her father's pulse. There was no pulse. She pumped his chest wall, but there was no sign of life. Her father was dead.

She ran frantically back into the bungalow, and, seizing the hall telephone, rang the emergency services. She told them what had happened, and noted the time of the call. She then slumped to the floor and wept. The police officer found her there, crying uncontrollably. He recognised her. A few seconds later the ambulance arrived. Together they rushed to the garage, and carefully pulled Buller out of the car. They carried him out of the garage, and laid him gently on the driveway. The ambulance men quickly checked him over. Buller was dead.

Elspeth had noticed the arrival of the police car and ambulance outside Buller's bungalow. She pulled on a coat, and rushed over to Buller's bungalow. There she saw the ambulance men leaning over Buller's body. Suppressing her tears, she ran into Buller's bungalow to see the policeman gently escorting the wailing Susan into the sitting room.

The police officer searched Buller's bungalow, whilst the forensic team searched the garage and the Ford Escort. On the kitchen table, the officer found an envelope addressed to Susan. Elspeth was nursing the distressed Susan on the sofa. The officer showed Susan the envelope. She invited him to open it. It read:

257

'My dearest Susan,

I am sorry but I cannot carry on. My life ended in Salcombe, and I see no future for me. In fact, I see my very existence as an obstacle to your future happiness. Graham Mitcham is a very fine and honourable man. He did what he had to do. He knew that he was risking his future with you, but he had no alternative. He will make a fine husband for you, and my continued existence prevents the two of you getting together. This is no instant decision on my part. I thought of little else whilst I was in prison, and my release has made no difference to my decision which I made a long time ago. I long for you to be happy, free from responsibility for me. I hope that you and Graham will get together again and marry, and both remember my wish that you do so.

Please give my love and apologies to Elspeth, and thank her for not deserting me. We enjoyed some wonderful times together. I have sent a copy of this letter to Graham, so that he knows my thoughts, and knows that I acknowledge that he did what he had to do, and that I admire him for it and certainly bear him no grudge. Quite the contrary. My dearest wish is that you two marry.

Do not grieve for me, Susan. I am happy that I am doing the right thing for me, for the three of us. God bless. I love you.

Your ever-loving father,
Dad xxxx'

The officer handed it to Elspeth. She read it, tears welling in her eyes. She gently passed it to Susan, who wept uncontrollably as she read it.

News of Buller's suicide spread quickly through Menston. The suicide of a leading, if now notorious, citizen made front page news in the Menston Daily Chronicle and was hourly reported on the local radio. Elspeth telephoned Miss Turvey at Buller & Mitcham to tell her of the sad news. Miss Turvey in turn told Mitcham. Mitcham was staggered. He did not even know that Buller had been released from prison. Miss Turvey told him that Buller had been freed a month previously. Mitcham stared sadly out of his office window, recalling all that had happened between them.

The next day Mitcham opened a letter addressed to him, marked "Private". It was from Buller. He wept.

Elspeth kept Miss Turvey informed of events. The Coroner's officer had asked her to identify the body, which she had found a distressing experience. Susan was in a distressed state, blaming herself for going to work and leaving her father to his own devices. The inquest had been formally opened and adjourned to a future date. The funeral was scheduled for a week's time at Saint Swithun's Parish Church in Menston with cremation to follow. There would be a wake in

259

the Church Hall following the funeral service. Elspeth had arranged the funeral service with Reverend Paterson as Susan was too distressed to handle it. Miss Turvey in turn informed Mitcham. Mitcham decided to close the office for the funeral service, and asked his partners and staff to attend the funeral service. He knew that some would wish to go, and was concerned that there may not be many people at the service. It would be some comfort to Susan if, at the very least, his firm was in attendance.

Mitcham agonised over writing a letter of condolence to Susan. He felt, he knew, that he had to send one to her. Not to do so would be a snub, and show a callous indifference to her bereavement and the memory of her father. Yet it would be false to eulogise about her father. Such a letter posed an opportunity for a rapprochement, but if wrongly sculpted could cause lasting damage between them.

Sitting at his desk, after the office had closed, Mitcham attempted several drafts. In the end, he decided to play it safe, and wrote.

'Dear Susan,
I was so sad to learn of your father's death. He was always very good and kind to me, and he will be a great loss to you. Please accept my deepest sympathy, and my warmest wishes.

Yours ever,
Graham Mitcham'

Mitcham arrived early at the Church. It was a large building, and he anticipated a small congregation. He would be noticeable, and he did not wish to be. Despite the assurances in Buller's suicide letter, he was very uncertain of Susan's feelings towards him. Would she be pleased to see him there paying his respects or regard him as the grim reaper revelling in her father's death? He doubted that she would think the latter of him, but she may still regard him as the key architect in the events leading to her father's suicide. He did not wish to cause her extra distress, and wanted to find a pew where he could see her and witness the funeral service without being noticeable.

He selected a pew, sat down and prayed for Buller. Slowly mourners filed in, and he was pleased to see a full turn out from his firm. Funeral music played. Flowers adorned the altar and pulpit.

After a while the Church bells tolled the sad chimes for a funeral service. Mitcham glanced around and noticed that the congregation was very small. Old friends, clients and acquaintances had stayed away. He realised that, despite his careful planning, his very presence was conspicuous if Susan looked in his direction. The vicar then entered the Church followed by the funeral cortège and then Susan, Elspeth and several distant relatives. Mitcham was shocked by Susan's appearance. Dressed in black, she was clearly distressed, her face gaunt, pale and tired. Mitcham's eyes never left her. He was aching to be by her side, to hold her arm, to comfort her. Although the distance between them was only twenty feet it seemed a chasm. He felt a trespasser.

The service was mercifully short. No eulogy was given. Just prayers and hymns. The pall bearers gathered to take the coffin away and the mourners, led by Susan, filed out. Mitcham stiffened as for a second Susan's eyes locked on to him. 'Was that a small smile of recognition?' he wondered, as the moment passed, and Susan moved on.

Mitcham did not go to the wake. He did not want his presence to interfere with the party. He felt that his presence may not be welcome, would in any event be intrusive. What could he say to Susan? What could she say to him? How could they talk together? Would she want to talk to him? How would he feel if she ignored him, or dismissed him with a steely nod of her head or a curt reply? No, there was nothing to be gained and a lot to lose by attending. Susan, no doubt. would be thinking the same, perhaps dreading his attendance. If there were to be a meeting between them, a meaningful meeting, it had to be at a future time, a different place, a different atmosphere. He filed quietly out of the Church, and slipped away from the gathered throng, back across the Market Square to the office. There was work to be done.

All her misgivings about holding a wake after the funeral in case she met Mitcham were to no avail. Susan had worried about how she would meet Mitcham, what she would say to him, how they would disengage from one another, and would such disengagement prove to be final. She was terrified in case it all went wrong. Sleepless nights had concentrated on that fear. But now that the time had come, Mitcham was not there. She scanned the room in nervous apprehension, but he was not there. Relief accompanied disappointment. Instinctively and intuitively she understood and recognised that she was still in love with him, that she wanted her future to be with him. That without him there would be no future: no happiness, no fulfilment, no love. She returned home from the wake alone, aghast, and wretchedly miserable. A lonely future beckoned.

Weeks passed. Elspeth kept Miss Turvey informed about Susan, who in turn told Mitcham. Mitcham did think about contacting Susan, particularly to respond to the overture in Buller's suicide letter, but it was clear from the information that he was receiving from Elspeth, via Miss Turvey, that Susan was still in mourning, not coping at all well with her bereavement. Now was too soon, he felt. Susan returned to work, but her heart was not in it.

Mitcham did not attend the adjourned Inquest. He learned later that it had been a short formal affair. The Coroner's Officer had given evidence of what his findings were. The police officer told the Coroner that he had attended the deceased's house and described what he had found and produced Buller's suicide letter, which the Coroner had required him to read out. Susan had been called to describe her discovery of Buller's body, and her father's mood since his release from prison. No evidence to the contrary was given. The Coroner had then invited the jury to record a verdict of suicide whilst the balance of Buller's mind was disturbed. The jury had duly done as directed.

CHAPTER TWENTY-THREE

1986

Six months passed. Mitcham thought continually about Susan, wishing that he could be with her, to comfort her, to assuage her grief, and to renew their love. Often, he was tempted to write again to her, but was uncertain what to write, fearful that whatever he did write might cause Susan to be upset. He toyed with the idea of asking Elspeth to set up a reunion or a party to which both he and Susan would be invited, but the fear of rejection made him desist. Frustration ruled the day. There seemed to be no solution: he could only hope that chance one day would reintroduce them to one another.

Susan thrust her energy into her career. It was the only practical way that enabled her to cope with her grief. Absorption in her work took her mind away from her loss and the tragic sequence of events that had caused it. But she could not erase from her mind the horror of discovering the suicide of her father. It disturbed her sleep, often causing her to awake from a nightmare in a feverish sweat. And she longed to be reunited with Graham, to be in his arms again and to renew her love for him. But she also knew that, in such reunion, it was inevitable, indeed unavoidable, that they would discuss her father's crimes and the part that Graham had played in revealing them.

Whilst she was curious to learn all the detail of the unravelling of her father's crimes and the pressures that had enveloped Graham, at the same time she recoiled from any defamation of her father that such discussion would involve. So, reunion with Graham was a poisoned chalice, one that enthralled her yet frightened her; one that she was too wounded to undertake, let alone pursue. Her evenings and weekends at home were dominated by grief, and remorseless preoccupation with morbid thoughts about the dilemma of meeting Graham. She could find no peace, no comfort, no solace. Long discussions with her friends provided no answer. Elspeth sought to comfort her, but to no avail. Work was the only respite, the only escape.

In a chance encounter in Menston one lunchtime, Susan learned from Miss Turvey that Mitcham was still living in the house in Manley Road which they had chosen together. Miss Turvey talked to her about personalities at the office, but Susan's attention had drifted elsewhere. That evening she surreptitiously drove along Manley Road and slowly passed the house, hoping yet fearing that she would catch sight of Graham. But he was not to be seen. Relief that she had been spared the dilemma of what she would do if she had seen him was torn by sadness that she had not seen him. She turned the car round at the end of the road, and slowly drove back along the road, gazing anxiously at the house. But he was not to be seen. The house looked deserted and forlorn. Tears

266

welled up in her eyes until she could hold them no
more, and, as she drove back to her bungalow, she
broke down in tears and wept desperately all the way
back. The visit had proved a heartache, and, worse,
she felt that she was behaving like a stalker. She
resolved sadly never to repeat the experience.

March 1986

Mitcham was looking forward to going to the County
Law Society's Annual Dinner that evening. He had
not been to one for several years, still feeling slightly
embarrassed by Buller's misbehaviour. But that
chapter was now mercifully closed, and Mitcham had
begun to enjoy life again. He felt more at ease. He
tied his bow tie, looked at himself in the mirror,
decided that all was in order and left his bathroom. A
few minutes later he was driving his car slowly
towards the town centre, in no hurry, relaxed and
enjoying the classical music being played on the car
radio. A lovely evening beckoned.

Susan was seated in her car, about to leave the
Surgery car park, when a call came through to her on
her emergency radio. "There has been a road traffic
accident at the Hills Road/ Grafton Street junction.
Please proceed immediately. One person is believed
to be dead, the other in a critical condition." Susan
pursed her lips, set her lamp flashing and her car's

267

clarion wailing, and sped off.

Three minutes later, she entered Hills Road and
noticed a police car parked across the road at the
Grafton Street junction, its blue light flashing. A
crowd of people had gathered. She parked her car
next to the police car, grabbed her medical bag and
ran to the scene of the accident. She could see a
motor bike embedded in the driver's door of a Jaguar
motor car. A body lay on the ground. It appeared
lifeless. She stopped by it, knelt down and felt the
pulse. There was none; the motor cyclist was clearly
dead. "Over here doctor," called the police officer.
"This one is alive. The ambulance is on its way."
Susan ran over to the passenger side of the car. The
door lay open. She started to climb into the passenger
seat. She froze. The driver was slumped back in his
seat belt, looking white faced, and asleep. It was
Graham.

Subduing her pain of discovery, she moved over to
Graham and felt his pulse, which, to her relief, was
strong. Graham groaned. She gently examined him,
and then opened her medical bag to administer an
injection to ease his pain. Graham's eyes opened
briefly as she inserted the needle, and gazed on
Susan. "You are going to be all right, Graham.
Nothing that a few weeks of recuperation will not put
right. The ambulance is on its way." Graham
nodded, and slipped back into unconsciousness.
Susan loosened his bow tie to ease his breathing and
gently caressed his brow. Mitcham came around
again, dreaming of screeching brakes, an agonized,

haunting scream and the noise of a big bang at his side. He agitated, and groaned as pain shot down his right -hand side. He could not move, he was strapped in. He sought to release himself, but could not move his right arm. He was imprisoned. He felt the restraint of a hand, and then looked uncomprehendingly at Susan. "Where am I?" he asked. "What's happened? Susan, why are you here? What are you doing here?" Susan smiled adoringly down at him. "There, take it easy, Graham. You are safe. You will be all right. Just relax. The ambulance will be here shortly."

Mitcham subsided again into unconsciousness. Regaining consciousness, he saw the smiling, reassuring face of Susan. Susan bent over him and gently kissed him on the lips. "Let's get married," Graham murmured. Tears welled up in her eyes. "Yes. Let's," replied Susan excitedly. "I love you. I have always loved you. I always will love you." Mitcham drifted back into unconsciousness, a smile on his face. The clarion noises of the ambulance and the fire engine announced their arrival. Susan kissed his forehead, and then carefully detached herself from Mitcham and climbed out of the car.

"Do you always kiss your patients?" demanded the police officer reprovingly. "Only when the patient is my fiancé," was her tart reply, to the astonishment of the police officer.

THE END

APPENDIX

For those unfamiliar with Solicitors' Accounts' Rules I should explain that these are statutory and require all firms of solicitors to keep their own money separate from the money of their clients. This is an absolute rule, and no transgression is allowed, either by the Law Society which supervised the application of these rules in the period covered by this story, or by their successors, the Solicitors Regulation Authority.

The application of the Rules means that every firm of solicitors must keep two separate books of accounts. All clients' money must be held in clients account which has its own client Bank account. All money belonging to the firm must be kept in the office account which has its own office Bank account. In practice, every client has his or her own client ledger so that all payments into or out of that account can be entered and traced. The total sum of all the balances on the individual client accounts must always equal the sum held in the client Bank account. This is an absolute rule. If there is a shortfall on the client Bank account, the solicitor must immediately fund the shortfall out of his own money so that the client Bank balance equals the amount on the firms' client account.

Printed in Great Britain
by Amazon